MW01141843

Really-Truly Stories

DEDICATION

This book is affectionately dedicated to Pearl Clements Gischler, coauthor of our Oregon historical juveniles; and to the many friends whose stories appear in the "Really-Truly" books, especially: June Dalton Foster, Frances Donegan Williamson, The Hibbards, Sarah P. Ashbaugh, and Nicholas Schneider.

MARY MARTHA'S

REALLY-TRULY

STORIES

BOOK THREE

By

Gwendolen Lampshire Hayden

Illustrated by Vernon Nye

Review and Herald Publishing Association
Takoma Park, Washington, D.C.

Printed in the U.S.A.

**PRINTED IN
THE UNITED STATES OF AMERICA**

World rights reserved. This book or any portion thereof may not be copied or reproduced in any form or manner whatever, except as provided by law, without the written permission of the publisher, except by a reviewer who may quote brief passages in a review.

The author assumes full responsibility for the accuracy of all facts and quotations as cited in this book.

Facsimile Reproduction
As this book played a formative role in the development of Christian thought and the publisher feels that this book, with its candor and depth, still holds significance for the church today. Therefore the publisher has chosen to reproduce this historical classic from an original copy. Frequent variations in the quality of the print are unavoidable due to the condition of the original. Thus the print may look darker or lighter or appear to be missing detail, more in some places than in others.

2004 05 06 07 08 09 10 11 12 · 5 4 3 2 1

Copyright © 2004 TEACH Services, Inc.
ISBN-13: 978-1-57258-435-8
ISBN-10: 1-57258-435-1
Library of Congress Control Number: 2006927619

Published by

TEACH Services, Inc.
www.TEACHServices.com

CONTENTS

Hardly Six Inches From His Unprotected Face Hung a Huge
Indian Cobra

CHAPTER 1 | The Hooded Death

TOMMY WIPED his perspiring face, closed his eyes again, and vainly wished that he and his parents were sitting on a magic carpet, sailing quickly through the air to the Vincent Hill Station.

"We wouldn't even stop at Roorkee training school either!" he mumbled, sleepily jerking out his crumpled handkerchief to mop his damp forehead.

"What, dear? You don't want to stop at Roorkee and see our friends and little Maxine?" Mrs. Wallace asked. She leaned forward anxiously. "I wonder if you're feverish, Tommy. You have been muttering to yourself for the past hour. I wonder if you're going to be ill."

"Oh, no, nothing's wrong, Mother," sighed the boy, opening tired brown eyes. "I guess I was just thinking out loud. Of course I want to see Maxine and her folks. But—but it's just so *hot* down here on the plains. I can hardly wait until we get into the Himalaya Mountains, where I can really cool off."

Mr. Wallace patted his son's shoulder. "Try to sleep now. It'll help the time to pass more quickly. And no amount of wishing will hurry along this train or bring cool weather. You must remember that it will be two months before the monsoons (heavy rains)."

But Tommy learned that nothing lasts forever, not even extreme discomfort, for when at last he was roused he found to his joy that it was time to get off the train and greet the smiling friends who pushed forward through the colorful, teeming crowds to welcome this missionary family.

"My, but your house feels cool," he exclaimed grate-fully, as he laid down his knife and fork, and leaned back in his chair. It had been several hours since they had entered the Roorkee mission home, there to find bathing facilities and a delicious meal awaiting them. Tommy had especially enjoyed visiting at the table with little Maxine and hearing her tell about next week's Sabbath school lesson as she proudly recited her Bible memory verses.

Then the talk had again turned toward the weather. Tommy had stared at the dining room walls as he spoke.

"It's a good thing those walls are so thick," he volun-teered. "Even the hottest sunshine can't get through two feet of stone."

"That's true, Tommy," smiled his host. "These stone-and-masonry houses are purposely designed to keep out heat but still permit stray breezes to come in through the unglassed windows."

"Yes, and very conveniently let a snake crawl through their iron bars and open shutters!" added Mrs. Wallace with a little shiver. "Although I've lived in India for a number of years I have not yet conquered my fear of snakes, especially the cobra. Its bite is so deadly!"

Their hostess nodded quickly. "Yes, I feel as you do, but of course we can't give way to our fears. If we did, we would be unable to carry on our missionary visits, for snakes are prevalent here. However, we exercise all possible caution, especially at night, when we are careful never to walk on the grass or go without a flashlight, for we have seen many natives die quickly and horribly from the cobra's fatal bite."

Noting their interest, Mrs. Brown continued, "The most feared is the *cobra de capello,* or 'hooded terror.' The high-caste Hindus can hardly be persuaded to kill these dangerous snakes, even though their venomous bite is largely responsible for the 20,000 annual deaths attributed to snake bites here on our Indian peninsula. No doubt this is because the India cobra has been worshiped since the beginning of history.

"We've killed a number of them around our home, for since they feed on frogs, lizards, and small mammals which enter our more or less open dwellings here, they frequently come into the house. We have found that when a cobra is aroused it becomes very vicious.

"I'll never forget the first native I saw die from cobra venom. It was only a matter of a few minutes before he was gone, for the venom acts directly upon the nervous system. For a long time I was haunted by the picture of that yellowish-brown body partly raised, swaying to and fro as its eyes glared and its neck-ribs spread into the great spoon-shaped expansion called the hood.

"But come," she concluded, rising from the table.

"I know that you must be tired from your long journey. You'll no doubt be glad to rest. So if you'll come with me, I'll show you to your room now, while the men are gone to the study for a few minutes.

"Tommy, I'm sure that you won't mind lying on a cot in your parents' room for your afternoon rest. We've been redecorating the bedroom that you are to occupy, and the work is not quite finished. However, it will be ready for you by evening. Until then, your traveling bags have been put in your parents' room."

"Oh, no, I don't mind, Mrs. Brown," laughed Tommy, as he looked around the large bedroom. "Why, this guest room is big enough for five or six people."

"All right, then," nodded their hostess. "I'll call you after an hour or so. Until then do try to sleep. It will do you good."

She had scarcely turned away before Tommy had removed his socks and shoes, and had flung himself down on the narrow cot.

"My, but this soft bed feels comfortable after that jolting train ride," he sighed in contentment, as he stretched out on his back and gazed up at the ceiling. "I know that I'll be asleep in two winks. How about you, Mother? Don't you think a nap will cure your headache?" He looked anxiously at his mother, for he knew how painful were the headaches that quickly occurred whenever she became overtired.

Mrs. Wallace smiled wanly at her son. "I'm sure that rest will be a great help, dear. But first perhaps I'd better take some of that medicine that I brought along. There it is—in my small handbag. And I'll need a cup of hot water, Tommy. Would you mind asking Mrs. Brown for one?"

"Of course not, Mother," the boy answered. "I'll be glad to. Just a minute. I'll get my slippers out of my smallest suitcase over here. Let's see—where are they? Oh, I remember. They're in the tan bag on the chair by the doorway."

He straightened up quickly at the sound of excited shouts outside. They heard voices crying, "This way. Watch out! Careful now. Don't make a false move. No, over there. I'm sure it's over there. Be careful!"

"What do you suppose has happened?" stammered Mrs. Wallace. She half sat up in bed, only to fall back with a moan of pain.

"Oh, my head, my head!" she cried. "I can't even sit up. Hurry and get the hot water, dear. I won't be any better until I take my medicine, I'm sure."

"All right, Mother." Tommy answered. He hurried to the chair by the bedroom door and bent over the tan bag. He lifted out his new slippers and then leaned down to slip them on his bare feet. As he straightened quickly and stepped toward the door, an agonized whisper startled him.

"Tommy!" The cry shivered through him and rang knell-like in his ears.

"Tommy! don't move. Don't *move!*" For all its faintness the soft tone of his mother's voice throbbed in the air like a scream.

The boy stood transfixed with fear. Although he did not know the reason for the command, he unquestioningly obeyed his mother.

"Look!" Her voice shook with fright. "Look ahead of you. But don't move!"

His fearful gaze crept up the door casing. Up, up, up —his look moved ever so slowly, until at last he saw what his terrified mother had first seen as she watched him prepare to leave the room. There on the roughened door casing, hardly six inches from his unprotected face, hung a huge Indian cobra.

Its beady eyes stared unwinkingly into his. Its slimy coils inched upward, preparing to strike.

As Tommy discovered the reptile he felt as though he would faint. His heart seemed to leap and turn over in his breast; his knees quivered and scarcely held him up. He swallowed convulsively. Sweat broke out on his forehead as he helplessly clenched his fists.

"What shall I do? What can I do? I know I mustn't move," the speechless boy groaned inwardly. His thoughts ran round and round over the same sentences, like a phonograph needle caught in one groove on a record.

And over and over from the bed across the room came his mother's harsh whisper, "Don't move, Tommy. Don't move! If you value your life, don't move!"

The vivid description of the cobra Mrs. Brown had made at the table flashed across the boy's mind. Then, as in an awful dream, Tommy again heard his mother's gasping, "Don't move, son. Pray. Pray as you have never prayed before."

How could he pray? He dared not move as much as a muscle. He dared not kneel or bend his head or close his eyes. But how he prayed! Oh, how he prayed that moment as he stood face to face with the fearful hooded death. His cry for help burst forth from his anguished heart.

And as he prayed, the words of little Maxine's Bible texts seemed to flash like fire before his eyes.

"The angel of the Lord encampeth round about them that fear Him, and delivereth them."

"He that dwelleth in the secret place of the most High shall abide under the shadow of the Almighty."

"There shall no evil befall thee. . . . For He shall give His angels charge over thee, to keep thee in all thy ways."

The words rang over and over in his ears as the shouting outside came nearer and nearer, and hurrying footsteps rushed into the house.

"For He shall give His angels charge over thee, to keep thee in all thy ways"——"*in all thy ways.*"

"Why, this awful moment is one of *my* ways," Tommy thought. "And surely God can send His angels to save me *now*—right now, just as He has saved many others from death. Oh, please, dear Jesus, do save me!"

An uncontrollable trembling shook his rigid form as he pled with God. A strange feeling rushed through his tense body as frantic footsteps neared the door. Excited voices cried, "This way. It must have come into the house. We could find no sign of it outside."

At that very instant the cobra struck. Straight out into the air it hurled its loathsome coils, toward Tommy's face, not six inches from his unwavering eyes. And then —before the horrified, unbelieving gaze of the men and servants who stared in from the hall—the snake shot harmlessly past the boy's ear and fell with a loud thud in the middle of the room.

Tommy sank weakly to the floor as the men rushed forward. For a minute loud cries and the clatter of sticks and garden tools filled the air. Then all was silent as Mr. Wallace ran toward Tommy, gathered him in a close embrace, and hurried to the bed where Mrs. Wallace lay, white and trembling. Tommy clung to his father and mother while, unmoving and speechless, the three watched their friends carefully carry out the ugly, severed head and limp brown coils of the once deadly, but now harmless, cobra.

At last Tommy regained his voice. He looked into his mother's eyes and said, "I did just what you told me to do, Mother. I know that *that* was what saved my life."

"Indeed you obeyed, darling," Mrs. Wallace replied in a faint, quivering tone. "If you had moved even one inch the snake would have struck directly at you."

"Oh, but that wasn't what I meant, Mother——"

"But the cobra *did* strike directly at his face, my dear," Mr. Wallace's voice interrupted. "I stood in the doorway directly facing Tommy, and until I saw the expression in his eyes I was more terrified than I have ever been in my life."

"The expression in his eyes? I—I don't understand," faltered his wife. "What do you mean?"

"Yes, my dear," Mr. Wallace continued. "When I saw the light in Tommy's eyes I knew that our boy was indeed under the shadow of the Almighty, for it was as though he beheld a heavenly being there to care for him and to protect him. I am convinced that an angel stood between Tommy and the cobra, and that it was his presence that saved our boy from certain death."

Tommy gravely nodded his head. "You see, Mother, I did just what you told me to do. I said Maxine's Bible verses over and over, and I prayed as I had never prayed before. I learned that I didn't have to kneel down in church to ask God's help. I just asked Him right there to save me, and He did! All at once I knew that if I believed enough in His promises I'd be safe, and then it seemed to me that I wasn't afraid any more."

With joyful tears in his eyes Tommy smiled at his thankful parents as he added, "And I'm sure that my favorite Bible text is always going to be the one that I repeated over and over—'There shall no evil befall thee. . . . For He shall give His angels charge over thee, to keep thee in all thy ways.' "

Arrie Burst Open the Kitchen Door Before Her Father
Had Time to Spring to His Feet

CHAPTER 2

A Dinner
of Herbs

"OH, COME ON, Arrie. Do come home with me to-night and stay all night. I've coaxed and coaxed, but you've never spent a single night at our house, and I've stayed here lots of times."

Arrie's tightly braided red pigtails bobbed back and forth as she shook her head and smiled at her friend. As they talked they hurried down the long, muddy lane that led from the little country schoolhouse.

"I don't think I should ask mother to let me go, Jane. Really, I don't. I'm the oldest of all of us children and I'm a good deal of help with the housework after school. Mother really needs me."

"Oh, pooh!" sniffed Jane. "Let Sarah set the table tonight and dry the dishes. She's nine and only a year younger than you are. It'll do her good to take over some of the re-re-respon—what is that long word the bigger pupils had in spelling today?"

"Re-spon-si-bil-ity!" proudly answered Arrie, sounding out each syllable as the teacher had done.

"That's it," nodded her friend. "So just let her take some of the responsibility. She'd have to do it all the time if you got married."

The two little girls giggled merrily at the thought of ten-year-old Arrie marrying and leaving her Texas home and the younger brothers and sisters. But her freckled face sobered as they turned in at her gate and Jane continued to plead.

"Well, I'll really be cross with you if you don't let me ask your mother. Yes, I will, too! If you want to work so much you can help Mary and me do our chores. We always have to gather the eggs and carry up the milk pails for father." Her nose wrinkled with distaste. "Since he hasn't any boys in his family, we always get that sloppy old job. I just hate carrying a heavy milk bucket all the way from the barn. The path's slippery, and sometimes we almost fall down."

They clattered onto the back porch, wiped their muddy feet on a folded gunny sack, and entered the plain, neat, spicy-smelling kitchen.

"Why, hello, girls. I didn't expect you home quite so soon. How's my big girl?" Arrie's mother asked in her sweet voice, as she kissed Arrie and smiled at Jane.

"Please, Mrs. Bliss, can't Arrie come home with me and stay all night?" begged Jane. "This morning my mother said I should ask her, and if Arrie couldn't stay she wasn't going to let either Mary or me stay at your house any more. So please, please let her come, because we just love to stay here. It's lots nicer than it is at home."

Arrie looked in surprise at her school friend. She knew that the Hampton girls always enjoyed staying overnight with the Bliss family, but she couldn't imagine why they found it so much more pleasant than their own large house. Arrie's home was small but neat, even though crowded almost to bulging with seven children, mother, and father. Their furniture, plain enough when new, was now battered and scarred, though well polished, and their floors were scrubbed to a shining whiteness where not covered with worn carpet rag rugs. But Jane's house was filled with unbelievable treasures, even to a real parlor with velvet portieres, a flowered Brussels carpet, a marble-topped table that held a beautiful red-plush picture album, a carved whatnot, and—actually—a real organ. Oh, surely she must be mistaken in what Jane had just said.

She looked up in time to see her mother slowly nodding as she stirred a big kettle of simmering bean soup.

"Yes, I believe it may be best to let Arrie go with you this once," the surprised girl heard her mother reply. "However, I want both of you to hurry along and not be out after dark. There's been talk of a few thieving Indians around in the vicinity, and although I don't take much stock in the report, it's best not to run any risk. Have a nice time, dear, and be a kind, helpful girl," she finished, kissing Arrie good-by.

It seemed no time at all before Arrie found herself trudging the two miles down the lane to the Hampton house. She swallowed a lump in her throat as she recalled how the baby had clung to her skirts and cried as she pulled away. Baby was such a darling, with her big blue eyes and golden curls. She hated to be away from her during school hours, and she'd miss her even more over night. She'd miss all of them—Tom and Bob, Joe and Dick, Mary, and father and mother.

"Come on, now," teased Jane, as she looked at her friend's downcast face. "You're not going away forever, you know; it's just for one night, and then you'll be stopping tomorrow morning to put on a clean school dress. I'll race you to our kitchen door. Hurry up!"

It was fun to speed through the gate, up the path, and around the large house to the Hampton's kitchen door. Arrie began to lose her lonesome feeling as she entered the kitchen and to feel quite excited that she was going to stay all night in what her father had said was the biggest and most expensively built house in the entire country. She had been here on several previous occasions when her mother had called, but she had never been through all the rooms. Now she stared quite frankly as Jane escorted her from room to room and showed her the heavy, expensive furniture and the hair-wreath ornaments and crayon portraits on the walls.

Half an hour sped by before the girls heard a fretful call from downstairs.

"Jane. Jane Hampton! Where are you? Jane, answer me!"

"Oh, give me time and I will," Jane muttered under her breath, as she hurried to the top of the stairway and called down.

"We're up here, Ma. Did you want me?"

"We? Who's we?" the cross voice inquired.

"Why, Arrie, of course. Don't you remember? You

said she could come home with me tonight? Mary had to stay after school, and so we didn't wait for her."

Jane's voice rose in surprise, and Arrie's sinking feeling began to return.

"Oh! Well, to be sure, I said she could come and stay, and about time, too, I'd think, after all the evenings we've left you and Mary at her house while we were away on business. But come now. Just remember that you've chores to do even if you do have company. Arrie can sit down here in the parlor and look at the picture album if she's a mind to, but you've got work to do, young lady. I'm surprised that you haven't tended to the chickens. You know better than to fiddle-faddle away your time after school like this. I'll have to speak to your father again. I do declare, I never saw such irresponsible, lazy——"

On, on, and on the voice complained. It pursued them as they passed the chill and silent parlor, for Arrie shook her head to show that she would far rather help Jane with her chores than sit in there all alone. It carried relentlessly to their ears as they mutely went down the path to the barn, swinging the clean, shining milk pail between them. Even after they were out of hearing, the harsh tones rang in their memory.

"That's one reason why I like your house better than mine," soberly stated Jane. "You see, your mother's voice is always quiet and kind, and your father's voice is full of fun and laughter. I can't exactly explain—but it makes me all warm clear down inside just to see them and hear them talk. And you folks always have so much fun, too! No matter what you do, even work, you do it together, and it's fun! Our work is always just plain old work. We never do any chores together."

"Well, there you are at last," broke in Mr. Hampton's gruff voice as he took the milk pail. "I'd just about given up and decided I'd have to go to the house myself to get it, after being down here all afternoon with a sick cow—and one of my best milkers, at that. Go on, tend to the chickens while I milk, and mind that you hurry back to carry the milk up to the house. I'll be busy here."

Silently they fed and watered the noisy chickens and returned just in time to see Mary hurry into the barn.

"I'll help Jane carry the milk bucket, Arrie," she said breathlessly. "You can take the egg basket if you want to, but ma said most specially that you weren't to carry the milk, cause it might spill over on your good school dress. You see, Jane and I always change our clothes as soon as we come home so we can do our chores, and a few extra spots won't hurt these old dresses."

"Hoo-Hoo! Hurry up, you folks. Supper's ready," shrilled Mrs. Hampton from the back porch, cupped hands to mouth. "Come on before it's spoiled."

The three girls hurried up the muddy path toward the house. All at once Jane slipped. She struggled to right herself, and almost regained her balance, then slipped once again and fell, dragging the full milk pail with her. Half of the foamy white liquid sloshed onto the mud before Mary grabbed the handle and pulled the pail upright.

"Oh-oh-oh!" half-sobbed Jane as she struggled to her feet. "What will pa and ma say!" She and Mary stared fearfully at each other above the half-empty bucket. They did not have long to wait before finding out.

"You clumsy girls!" stormed their father. He rushed toward them from the barn. "Can't you ever learn to be careful? If you can't watch what you're doing, I'll teach you a lesson that will help you to remember."

He cuffed Mary and Jane—sharp, ringing blows that brought tears to their eyes.

"Now go along and get ready for supper. You know it makes your ma angry to wait after she calls us. She likes to eat early and get the work out of the way!"

Shrill exclamations and more cross words followed them, echoed by the petulant admonitions of Mrs. Hampton as they strained the milk, washed the pail, and prepared for supper.

"Here I've got a nice meal ready, and it'll all be cold before you sit down to eat a bite," wailed Mrs. Hampton, as they seated themselves at a table loaded with well-cooked food. "I work my fingers to the bone for you, and what thanks do I get? None!"

On and on flowed the bitter words, accompanied by an occasional assenting growl from Mr. Hampton. Arrie looked at the shining silver and glassware and the table loaded with delicacies, and contrasted it with the plain tableware and supper menu in her own home that evening.

In her mind's eye she saw their lamp-lighted, scarred old kitchen table covered with the gay red-and-white-checked tablecloth, with the blue bowls full of steaming, nourishing soup and the big kettle of hot cornmeal mush served with rich cream and honey. And she could almost hear her mother's soft, gentle voice as she said grace and her father's deep, kind response as he added, "Amen," then waited on each child in turn, beginning with the baby. What fun they would be having. Each one would have something of interest to tell—some incident of school or home—and even Baby would cry out "Me too. Baby talk too," and everyone would laugh.

Suddenly she lost her zest for the rich food before her. It would scarcely go down past the now big lump in her throat. For politeness' sake she tried to eat a few bites, but most of the food on her plate was left untouched when her hostess suggested that she go into the sitting room and rest while the girls carried out the dishes and "did" them.

Mrs. Hampton's voice floated back to Arrie as she gingerly sat down on the front edge of the plush platform rocker.

"Just look at all that food gone to waste, will you! Why, the child hardly ate anything. No wonder she's so skinny. No wonder her father's so poor! If Mrs. Bliss is as wasteful in all her cooking as that child is with her food, she'll always be poor and live in a wretched little house and have nothing."

Poor? A wretched little house? Have nothing?

Suddenly Arrie could not stay there a minute longer. An overpowering wave of homesickness swept over her as she thought longingly of that dear little home where love and contentment were all she had ever known and where courtesy toward one another was as commonplace as the air they breathed.

Poor? They had ample food and clothing.

A wretched little house? It was a happy, contented one.

Have nothing? Why, they had everything. They had each other!

She tiptoed out into the hallway, snatched her coat and bonnet, and slipped silently out of the big front door. As she closed it, the darkness pressed in upon her like a living thing, and she caught her breath. It was so very dark, and she seemed so very small. And then all at once she remembered that her mother had spoken about Indians! But, even though they might be near, she couldn't stay here. She just couldn't. She'd rather risk meeting a wild Indian than stay where people said such cross, hateful words to each other. Without hesitation she turned toward the gate and began to run.

On and on she sped, scarcely stopping for breath. She dared not look to the right or to the left, but steadily she walked and ran the long two miles, until at last she spied the faint glow of lamplight in their kitchen window. Per-

On She Ran Until at Last She Spied the Faint Glow of
Lamplight in Their Kitchen Window

haps—oh, perhaps they were still eating. They might have been later than usual, since she wasn't there to help. Oh, how she hoped that they were all sitting around that dear old table.

Arrie rushed across the porch and burst open the kitchen door before her father had time to spring to his feet.

Yes, they were! They *were* sitting around the big table, just as she had pictured them. It seemed as though she had been gone for years and years! With a cry she flung herself into her mother's lap and, as those tender arms closed around her, for the first time she began to sob.

"O Mother, I'm home again. I'm home," she choked, as mother's hand smoothed her hair, father patted her shoulder, and the children crowded close.

It was some time before she was ready for bed. Then, in her high-necked, long-sleeved nightgown and with mother's old red flannel robe across her shoulders, she sat at the table and ate with enjoyment her belated meal. She had not needed to say much to her parents. In the way of fathers and mothers the world round, they had understood her stammered words and halting sentences, and after the first questioning they had filled in the whole story.

"I really think you should saddle Betsey and go tell Mr. Hampton that Arrie's safe at home," mother said in a hushed voice after she had tucked Arrie in bed and given her a kiss.

"Yes, I was just going to do that very thing," she heard father say. "I'm more than sorry if he's been caused any worry or inconvenience. But I'm sure that he'll understand why Arrie ran away from their place after dinner was over. 'Better is a dinner of herbs where love is, than a stalled ox and hatred therewith.' Yes, I'm sure that he'll understand."

But then she slipped away into a contented, delicious slumber that closed out the sound of Mr. Hampton's anxious knock and the long conversation that followed between the three adults.

Arrie's first overnight visit to Jane's home was her last one. She had learned that home was such a happy place to be that there was no place on earth as dear, and until she grew up and married she was quite content to stay there and serve as mother's willing and trusted helper.

And even when Arrie was a sweet old lady over eighty years of age, the memory of that plain little love-filled home still brought tears of joyful remembrance to her eyes as she often told the story of how she ran away from the fatted ox, choosing instead a dinner of herbs.

CHAPTER 3

Indians!

ARAMINTA PATTED her sixth mud pie into a flat cake, sprinkled a pinch of white flour on top, and trimmed it with a tiny sprig of the syringa which grew in great clusters around the house.

"Mm-m-m! I certainly like the sweet smell of this mock orange, don't you, Belinda?" she asked her younger sister, who was busily stirring a can of mud batter.

"I certainly do. It's just about my favorite flower, except for the early spring yellowbells and bluebells. I wish I had some of them right now so that we could decorate the table for our tea party." Belinda gave her batter a final quick stir and poured it out into a varied assortment of cracked cups and saucers and pieces of once-fine china plates.

"Well," asserted Araminta, "there's no use wishing for any of those flowers, because spring is past for this year. I'm happy that it's June. The sun's so nice and warm, and the air smells like perfume now that the wild

28

roses are blooming. Why don't you go over to the picket fence and pull off some of those blossoms for your cakes? If you don't hurry, we won't have time to finish the tea party for our dolls. Mother wants me to go to the store pretty soon. She needs more sugar for her cake, and father forgot to bring some home last night."

As she spoke, Araminta propped up Matilda, her new kid doll with the real black hair and blue eyes, while Belinda lovingly smoothed out the dress of Annabelle, her china-headed doll with its painted black hair and pink cheeks.

The little hostesses and their doll guests sat down at the big flat rock that lay between the lean-to and the heavy wooden door to the hollowed-out cave in the mountain where welled up the cool spring that kept their butter and cream and milk fresh and cold on even the hottest summer days. When the Blakes had first come to the little settlement of Canyon City, they had selected this very site primarily because of the spring in this cave, abandoned by some unknown miner.

Mr. Blake had completed the excavation, had replaced the rotting timber supports with strong, new ones, and had put on two doors: one of wood and one of iron. Thus Mrs. Blake found ample use for her cool cellar, which held constant stores of dairy products, fruits, and vegetables. For all this happened long before the days of the electric refrigerator, and a housewife of 1878 was very thankful for the wonderful convenience of a cool cellar adjoining the lean-to used for summer cooking.

"Araminta, dear, I need you now," her mother called. "I'm almost ready to stir up the cake for the church social tonight, and I'm sure that I haven't enough sugar for my recipe. Run over to father's store, like a good girl, and bring back just enough of the brown sugar for today. We'll get a larger amount later. And also tell father to bring home a wooden box of soda crackers when he comes. I'm making a big kettle of soup, and the crackers will taste good with it. Let me see—oh, yes—ask if the pack train from The Dalles has come in yet. I need a number of articles."

Araminta's long braids swung back and forth as she skipped quickly down the dusty white road to her father's store. She liked to go to the store. An air of excitement always hung over the weather-beaten building, where red-shirted miners, pig-tailed Chinese, and blanketed Indians mingled and bartered for goods. She especially liked to watch the slow-moving, black-eyed Paiute Indians as they came in to trade beads and pine gum for bread and meat, colorful bandanna handkerchiefs, and big blankets. It always amused her to see them immediately go outside with their purchases, spread out the new robes, and lie down to sleep in the store's shade.

She wondered why none of the usual lounging figures were outside the building today. She hurried into the coolness of the general store, with its tantalizing, mingled aroma

She Hurried Into the Coolness of the General Store

of pickles, cheese, calico, coal oil, leather boots—all the varied articles needed in a small mining community more than two hundred miles from the nearest source of supply.

Araminta walked quietly over to the counter and stood there without speaking until her father finished waiting upon a huge, black-bearded miner. As she gave him her mother's grocery order he unsmilingly handed her the articles before he spoke.

"Tell mother that the church social has been called off, Minta. Now, now, child, there's nothing to worry about, I'm sure. Just tell her that I'll try to be home around six o'clock, and I'll talk to her then. It might be a good idea for her to go ahead with her baking, though. We may need some of it sooner than we think!"

He turned away toward a jolly Irishman while Araminta gathered up her groceries and walked thoughtfully out of the door, glancing curiously at the little group of earnest, serious-faced men in front.

"I can't imagine why the social's been called off!" exclaimed Mrs. Blake. "Why, we've been planning it for weeks, and all the women have been cooking and baking for several days to be ready for it. Well, when father comes home he'll tell us the reason. But in the meantime I might as well go ahead and mix up my sponge cake, since I'd planned on doing so.

"Oh, good," shouted Araminta and Belinda in chorus. They enjoyed every dish prepared by their mother, who was an excellent cook, but best of all the desserts they liked the delicious sponge cake for which their mother was famous at church suppers—a fluffy, twenty-egg cake made with brown sugar and baked in her largest milk pan.

The two girls were sound asleep when their father finally reached home, and they did not hear their mother's exclamation of dismay as she hastily put down the new gray wool dress that she was finishing for Araminta to wear to Sunday school the next day.

Araminta roused just enough to hear her mother protest, "Oh, no, John. It can't be as bad as all that. Why, the old chief was here in town not long ago, right in your store." But the rest of the conversation died away as she again lapsed into slumber, and by morning she had quite forgotten the incident as she and Belinda awoke.

Early though it was, the summer morning was already warm when Araminta and Belinda jumped out of bed and hurriedly washed their hands and faces in the cold water in the big china washbowl on the corner commode. Quickly they dressed in their rickrack-trimmed muslin underwear and petticoats, their long stockings and black pumps, and then carefully put on the new gray wool dresses that mother had finished hemming the evening before. As they slipped their calico aprons over their heads and ran out to have their hair combed, they sniffed the good smell of waffles cooking on the iron waffle iron that fitted tightly down into the lidless hole on top of the wood range.

"Oh, waffles!" gleefully exclaimed Belinda. "How I do like waffles! I'm hungry right this minute for some."

"Well, then, dear," laughed mother, "hurry and set the table. And get one of the glass pickle jars filled with some of that apricot jam I canned last year. It'll taste

He Rushed by Them Shouting, "Into the Tunnels for Your Lives!"

good. And Minta, the porridge is almost ready. Will you please run out into the cellar? Get the smallest milk pan there, and bring it in, so that you can skim off the cream on top. But do be careful of your new dress. Don't spill milk on it. It'll make a grease spot."

Although Araminta hurried she took good care to follow her mother's advice. Indeed she wouldn't spoil her lovely wool dress that had been so carefully made. Why, Canyon City ladies used to beg her mother to make their dresses, for she was a skillful seamstress. Minta

3

loved to peek into the parlor when they came and brought the lovely lengths of grosgrain silk, so stiff that it stood alone, or yards and yards of pretty flowered calico, which they had purchased at father's store for one dollar a yard. And how she and Belinda loved to see them count out the four five-dollar or two ten-dollar gold pieces in payment for each dress. Yes, indeed she would take care of her new Sunday dress.

Breakfast over, the sisters hurried down the dusty road to Sunday school. The first bell began tolling just as they stepped off their wide veranda, but they knew that they would reach the church in plenty of time. All too soon the classes were dismissed, and they started on the return trip home, loitering along the way with a group of other girls.

Araminta, a few steps ahead of the others, had just turned the corner of the Gunlach store when she saw a man riding madly up the main street. By that time her companions had all reached her side. They stared in terror as the foam-covered horse galloped nearer and nearer.

"Oh, Minta, what's he yelling?" Belinda half-whispered, clinging to her older sister. "I'm scared, Minta. I'm scared most to death."

Now they saw that the rider was Joe Combs. He waved his hat over his head and shouted at the top of his voice as he rushed by them. "Into the tunnels for your lives, folks. Into the tunnels, everyone. Hurry! The Indians are coming!"

The Indians! Instantly Araminta knew why she had not seen any of the familiar blanketed figures loitering near the store for several days. She knew now why Father had looked so worried yesterday when he told her that the church social had been postponed.

"Quick, Belinda," she gasped. The girls turned toward their home and ran as they had never run before, braids streaming in the wind, broad-brimmed and ribbon-tied hats flapping up and down on the backs of their necks, full skirts held knee high. Breathlessly they clattered across the veranda and rushed into the house just as their father ran toward them from the store.

"To the mining tunnels," he shouted. "Hurry, Mother, grab some food and let's be on our way. We haven't a minute to lose. Joe Combs escaped from the battle at Dayville and brought word here. He says there are a thousand Indians on the warpath, and they're coming fast toward us.

"All the men who aren't acting as scouts are up on the hills digging rifle pits and building breastworks around the entrances to the mining tunnels, where the women and children are to be placed for safety. I want to be sure that you're up there before I get my shovel and gun, and join them."

Araminta looked frantically around. What should she take? Food? Clothing? Her doll! Of course Matilda must go and so must Belinda's china-headed Annabelle. But her feet seemed rooted to the floor. She stood still, almost paralyzed with fright until mother's calm voice spoke as quietly as though she were serving at the church social and asking if anyone wished another slice of cake.

"Of course, we'll go to the tunnels, John. It would be foolish not to do so. But first I'm going to store some of my best furniture out of sight of those wild Indians."

"Furniture?" croaked father, and the girls saw him turn and look at mother as though he thought she had taken leave of her senses.

"Furniture? You're thinking of furniture at a time like this, when we're all likely to be scalped right on the spot? Wife, you must have lost your mind."

"Be that as it may, I'm not going to walk out of here, John Blake, and just leave everything for those redskins to burn," his wife firmly replied. "I've worked too hard to go away and simply leave it all here for them to destroy."

"But, Mother," wailed Araminta, already feeling in imagination the clutch of a warrior's hand grasping her long hair. "Where can we put everything? There isn't any place to store it all."

"Oh, but there is, young lady," nodded tight-lipped mother. "We'll carry our best things out to the cellar and lock both doors. It'll take anyone some time to get through that outer one, I'll warrant. Here, John, let's start with the horsehair settee. Girls, you carry out the good chairs. Quick now!"

Tugging and straining, puffing and panting, they at last managed to hide most of the valued articles in the cave. But even then mother would not leave without taking food and several blankets. "No telling how long we'll have to be there, and we might as well eat and sleep with some degree of comfort." Araminta glanced wonderingly at her mother and thought in amazement that she didn't seem half so excited as her father did. Then

Fearfully They Toiled Up the Steep Mountain Slope
to the Tunnel

she saw the big milk pan full of cake go into the huge
hamper that they were using to carry their provisions,
and she had time to be glad that she had gone to the store
for the brown sugar needed in its baking.

At last they were on their way, hurrying down the
road, past frantic farm women who had heard the alarm
and had ridden desperately on horseback for the com-
parative safety of the little settlement of eight hundred
people. The girls stared with frightened eyes at some of
the crying, praying women who stood here and there in
forlorn little groups, hair shaken loose from their wild
ride, flour from their interrupted baking even yet dust-
ing their hands and clothing. They caught snatches of
breathless talk as they hastened by.

". . . killed all the large mares and colts, and drove
off all the horses. . . . burned seven homes at Long Creek.
I saw them burning. It was terrible."

Araminta wondered fearfully as they toiled up the steep mountain slope if they would ever reach the tunnel and the many friends who had already reached its safety. But, knees trembling from weariness, they at last found themselves high above the little canyon. As soon as they were safely inside the old mine, Mr. Blake left, and then the women crowded close together and laughed and cried as they compared the contents of their baskets and bundles. The Byrams found that they had excitedly wrapped up their custard pies in their bedding, and the Metschans learned that they had left their custard pies at home but had brought the roast instead. Mrs. Blake seemed to be the calmest one present. She told the girls to stay close to the tunnel entrance, out of sight of any prowling Indian scouts.

All day more and more settlers kept pouring in from outlying ranches. Araminta thought she had never seen anyone so busy as her mother, who hurried from group to group, helping to soothe a cross baby or to comfort a frightened young mother.

Araminta and Belinda acted as cook's helpers for the women who prepared the evening meal from the combined supplies. It was decided that it would be best to pool their resources, for some had brought nothing but bread, others had brought butter and crackers, and others had brought pies, cakes, roasts, or dried fruit. They carried water from the big tubs that the men had filled and placed just outside the tunnel entrance. And they kept a sharp lookout, along with all the others present, for any sign of approaching Indians.

At last everyone was settled for the night. Crying

babies had been stilled, and even the hushed voices of
the women had quieted before the two girls curled up
close to their mother on the single blanket spread on the
hard ground and finally managed to sink into a fitful
sleep.

After several days of worry and false alarms a scout
brought word that the Indians, upon learning that the
town was prepared for a surprise attack, had decided
to go around the mountain and not come down Canyon
Creek after all.

The girls listened fearfully to his account of the
Indians' journey across the country.

"At one ranch they murdered the owner's nephew,"
he stated solemnly. "Murdered him and burned the
home. The only things we found left were the feather
beds, which had been ripped open, and a forlorn
molasses-covered cat which had been stuffed down into
the feathers.

"They killed all the stock that they couldn't corral—
even took the old family clock apart. There wasn't a
thing left undone wherever they struck. It's lucky for us
that we didn't have them swoop down here."

"Then if the Indians have gone on, I'm going home,"
Mrs. Blake announced firmly some time after the messenger had departed. "There's no sense sitting up here in this
dark mining tunnel when my comfortable house is right
down there in the canyon in plain sight. It fairly makes
me homesick just to look at it. No, Mrs. Byram, I won't
be any more frightened there than I've been up here, for
every night I've wondered if maybe the Indians wouldn't
build a fire and smoke us out. Or else I've thought that

perhaps that big rock right up there over our heads in the roof of the tunnel might come crashing down on us. No, I'll surely be glad to get home. I expect that John will see us coming down the hill, and if so, he'll be at the gate to meet us."

It did not take as long for them to go down the steep hill as it had taken to struggle up the slope. Soon they had passed the huts and the mine waste piles along the creek, picking their way with care around the great heaps of rocks, pebbles, and sand where the rattlesnakes lay to sun themselves. But as they neared the familiar gate, Araminta glanced down at her new wool dress for the first time since their exciting departure from home. She was horrified to see that it was stained and bedraggled, spotted with milk and water, and blackened in several spots with soot from the cooking kettles. A quick glance at Belinda's dress proved it to be equally damaged.

"My new dress," wailed Araminta. "Look at my new wool dress, Mother. It's ruined! And all because of those Indians! And Belinda's dress is ruined too. Just look at my lovely new dress. And I tried so hard to keep clean."

Belinda began to sob and Araminta blinked back her tears and wished that she were not too old to give way and cry with her.

"Never mind, girls," said mother. "You worked faithfully while we were in the tunnel, and you couldn't help getting dirty. We're all a sight to behold, I must say. Now, as soon as we get in the house we'll build up a good hot fire in the cook stove, heat up a wash boiler full of water, and bring in our biggest round tin tub. Then we can each bathe and change our clothing.

"Later on I'll make each of you a new wool dress. We'll clean the ones that you are wearing, and then you can pack them away in moth balls, if you like, and keep them to show to your grandchildren as souvenirs of the Paiute-Bannock War of 1878." She smiled down at the dirty, bedraggled children as Belinda dried her tears and Araminta's face brightened.

Never had the white picket fence looked so spotless or the wide veranda so inviting as it did just then.

"Oh, but it's good to be home," cried Araminta when they entered their house and found father there to meet them. She gave him a hug and kiss, and then left him talking to mother as she ran into the parlor to see if the new Mason-Hamlin organ was safe. Then, as her eyes fell upon the sampler and its familiar motto, "HOME, SWEET HOME," which she had so carefully worked for mother's Christmas present the year before, she exclaimed:

"It's really true. I never realized it so much as I do right now. But it really is true. 'Be it ever so humble, there's no place like home.' "

Chief Egan Had Led the Indians Through the Bear Valley Country

CHAPTER 4 *Locked in a Mountain*

I T'S GOOD to be home again, isn't it, Belinda!" said Araminta. Her younger sister nodded as they threw the kitchen scraps to the greedy chickens and filled their clean empty tin with sour milk.

"My, I certainly got tired up there in that old mining tunnel. At first it was fun, in a way, because we saw so many children who live out of town. But I was scared too!"

"So was I," confessed Belinda. "I was just sure that the Indians would come any minute, yelling and whooping, and waving their tomahawks, all ready to scalp us!"

As the girls gathered the eggs and then put them in the big cool cellar in the mountainside, they glanced happily about. Never had the grass looked so green or the flowers so bright as they did in the warm June sunshine. Never had the bird songs sounded so sweet as now, with the tiny songsters swaying gaily in the branches of the tall, leafy trees.

It seemed hard to believe that only a few days before they and many other frightened settlers had huddled together in the dark tunnel that lay near the top of the mountain directly across from their home. It seemed hard to believe that there had been a bloody battle fought at Silver Creek in near-by Harney County and that Chief Buffalo Horn had taken refuge in a cave, where he was found after the battle, lying dead among his warriors.

News of the Paiute-Bannock War of 1878 had been brought to Canyon City by hard-riding scouts. The girls had listened wide-eyed and breathless to the news as the excited men discussed events with their father in his store.

"I always did say that Chief Buffalo Horn and his Bannocks would be up to no good," stated one travel-stained messenger. "He was smart enough to get guns and ammunition at Fort Hall. He thought he could persuade the Indians of Oregon, Washington, and Idaho to help him drive all the white people in these three States across the Mississippi River. But he was not so smart a warrior as old Chief Joseph of the Nez Percés. That chief fought the whole United States Army of the West, and when he surrendered, it was with all the honors of war!"

"No, Chief Buffalo Horn made a mistake by being jealous of Joseph," added another speaker. "And he paid for his mistakes with his life, after he'd plundered and killed all the way across southwest Idaho and into eastern Oregon. I'll always hold the murder of those two brave Smyth men of Happy Valley as a black mark on his record. The Smyths were friends of mine. They never had a chance—ambushed in their ranch house, driven out when it was set on fire, and shot down in their yard. I call it downright inhuman treatment!"

"It is," the girls heard father say gravely. "It *is* inhuman, and yet we must remember, men, that the Indian firmly believes that he is fighting for the right to occupy his own land, which he says the white man has taken from him. I don't hold with all this murder and theft, and I'll be the first one to fight if they come back, but just the same the Indians aren't altogether to blame. They haven't always been treated well by the white people, either."

"Defend the varmints if you will, John Blake, and speak kindly of them," interrupted the first man, shaking his head, "but I'll take my chances speaking to them from behind that old army needle gun of mine. It's got a four-inch cartridge and a kick like a mule, and it can deliver my message in a right smart way."

Hand in hand the girls had run home for reassurance and comfort from their mother.

"O Mother, do you think the Indians will come back?" Araminta had asked anxiously, following her mother's brisk step from room to room.

"No, dear, I'm sure they won't. Everyone has come home from the tunnels now, and scouts are constantly on duty on all the surrounding mountains, so that we need not be afraid of a surprise attack. No, I'm sure that we're safe. We learned that Chief Egan, who took command when Buffalo Horn was killed, had led the Indians through the Bear Valley country, down Murderers' Creek, and along the John Day River. Now he is on his way toward Pendleton. So I'm sure they won't return, especially since they know that our town is well defended.

"Now run on out and feed the chickens, and then you may play in the yard until I call you. I'm planning an extra good dinner—stewed chicken and dumplings is your father's favorite dish, you know. Then later on today we will move our furniture back from the cellar. The danger's past now, and I don't want to leave my nicest things there any longer than necessary."

And so Araminta and Belinda played happily with their dolls under the mock orange and wild rose bushes until they saw father coming down the dusty road. Then they sprang to meet him, their long flowered calico dresses flaring out as they ran.

"Well, well, how are my girls today? Feels pretty good to be home safe and sound, doesn't it?" he laughed down into their happy faces.

"Come on now. Let's go in and see if dinner's ready. Something smells mighty tasty to me!"

Dinner was ready and smoking hot on the table, for mother had seen the three hungry people coming along the road.

How good everything looked to Araminta as she stood by her chair, waiting for mother to sit down. Her eyes sparkled as she looked at the round dumplings swimming in rich broth, the mound of fluffy mashed potatoes, with a well of yellow butter on top, freshly baked bread, tomato preserves, green peas in cream sauce, a pitcher of ice-cold milk, canned peaches, and mother's three-egg sponge cake with pulverized sugar on top.

She and Belinda looked at each other and crinkled

their eyes in delightful anticipation. Araminta felt that she couldn't wait to take a bite. They sat down quietly and bowed their heads while father said grace. Then, plates filled with good food, they had just lifted their forks to take their first bites, when—

"Boom!" The sound shattered the quiet midday stillness.

"Oh!" gasped Araminta. Her fork clattered unheeded to the floor as she stared at her parents, who by now had run to the window. Another shot sounded farther up the canyon, and then another, while wild shouts arose from every side.

"Indians! Indians! Run for your lives."

Quickly they ran out onto the veranda and looked out from their narrow canyon across the open valley. Far in the distance huge dust clouds arose here and there across the level plain.

"Sure enough!" gasped father. "They're coming back, galloping as fast as they can. Good thing the scouts gave warning, or we'd have been trapped for sure. Hurry, folks. Gather up what you can while I lock up the barn and sheds. May not do much good, but it may be of some help."

Araminta did not stop to hear her mother say, "Oh, John, be sure to lock the iron door on the cellar. All our best furniture is still in there, for which I am thankful. So lock it up while I gather up what food we can take with us. Belinda, you and Minta go and get your coats and a blanket apiece. The nights are chilly in this high altitude, even if it is June."

Araminta flashed out the back door, through the

lean-to, and into the cellar. How dark it was after the bright sunshine. Somewhere in its coolness lay her doll, just where she had put her down this morning, when she ran in on an errand for mother.

"Where, oh, where are you, Matilda darling?" she asked breathlessly. "Did I leave you back by the spring?" She edged carefully around the piles of furniture and groped down by the spring to see if her beloved doll lay there.

"Here you are!" she exclaimed. "I've found you. Now we'll hurry and go back to the house. The Indians are coming, Matilda. We'll have to run!"

"Bang!" A loud noise shattered against her eardrums as she raised up, and at the same instant a smothering blackness enveloped her as she looked toward the doorway. No daylight was now visible. She could see nothing

Somewhere in the Coolness of the Dark Cellar
Lay Araminta's Doll

but the velvety darkness, hear nothing but her own quick breathing and the tiny trickle of the quiet spring.

"Locked in the mountain!" the thought flashed across her mind. "I'm locked in a mountain!" Araminta screamed and began to claw her frantic way toward the door. What had once been a friendly, familiar cellar had all at once become a frightening, mysterious place. Her teeth chattered and her knees shook together as she inched her way forward.

At last! She fell against the inner door's wooden surface and beat against it with frantic strength.

"Father! Father!" she called. "Let me out. Please let me out! It's Araminta. I'm in here. O Father, come and get me, please!"

But no sound penetrated that thick wooden door or the thicker iron one on the outside. And at last Araminta knew that she was really locked in! She thought sobbingly that even Indians on the warpath would not be as terrifying as was that black cave.

Suddenly she felt her head whirling round and round. Stars seemed to shoot across her eyes, a roaring sound grew louder and louder in her ears, and then all at once she fell in a little twisted heap on the floor and knew nothing more.

When she opened her eyes she stared wildly about her. The daylight seemed dazzling, and at first she could scarcely bear the faint light in the half-darkened bedroom.

"Where—where am I?" she gasped. She looked at mother and father and Belinda as though she had just returned home from a long journey.

"I—I don't remember what—oh, yes—the Indians—and the cellar. O Father," she stammered, and then two big tears slid out of her eyes and rolled down her pale cheeks as she looked at each dear face.

"There, there, child! Don't try to talk. You're going to be all right now," soothed mother's kind voice. She bent over, and with a clean linen handkerchief dried Araminta's wet eyes. "For several days you've been ill from your fright, but the doctor said that as soon as you awoke you'd begin to regain your strength."

"Yes, daughter," added father gravely. "I'll never forgive myself for closing and bolting that iron door when you were in the cellar. But as it happened, a number of folks came by just at that time to go to the tunnel, and in all the excitement and confusion we just supposed that you were in our group. We saw Belinda running here and there with the little girls and took it for granted that you were with her."

"Yes, and I thought you were with mother and father," added Belinda soberly. "It was awful when we got up there in the tunnel and found that you were missing. Father was so anxious to find you that he got down the hill almost in one jump!"

"But the Indians"—whispered Araminta, only now beginning to realize that she was really safe in her own bed in her own home, with Matilda on the bed beside her.

"That loud boom that we heard was not Indian gunfire after all," her mother stated. "The sheriff accidentally dropped his gun in the street. When it discharged, everyone within hearing distance was sure that the Indians had crept past the sentries and had begun firing on the town. Then others took up the alarm at once. We were all so excited that we believed the dust clouds in the valley were caused by the main body of Indians galloping rapidly toward us. But in reality they were caused by nothing more exciting than stock out in the pasture!"

"So our trip to the tunnel didn't last very long this time," Belinda hastily added. "And wasn't I glad!"

"Yes, we were all thankful that this was a false alarm. And we are even happier that our little girl is going to be all right after such a dreadful fright. This family has had enough excitement within the past few days to last a lifetime, I'm sure," stated father.

"Indians and tunnels and cellars!" murmured Araminta, her cheeks beginning to flush a pale pink as she fully realized that all was well.

"I guess I'll have a story to tell people," she murmured softly. "Won't folks be surprised when they ask me where I was when they thought the Paiutes were coming to Canyon City? I can just see their faces when I say, 'Where was I? Oh, I was hidden in a safe place where the Indians couldn't find me. *I* was locked in a mountain!'"

CHAPTER 5   "*Stay-Alive*
Johnny"

MAY I GO over and get Douglas now, Mother?" begged Johnny, as he took his last bite of breakfast. "We want to hunt some more bears today. We caught a big one yesterday afternoon and put him in the garage behind Douglas's house. Oh, how he growled at us when we led him across the street."

"What an imagination!" teased his big brother Tom. "Are you sure you didn't catch several bears? You really need two, and then each of you little boys would have a nice shaggy playmate. Think how cozy and warm he'd be in the wintertime, as he snuggled down on the foot of your bed! And wouldn't he make a nice, fluffy rug to stand on while you dressed?"

"Hush, Tom," spoke up mother. "I well remember when you were four years old. You didn't catch any bears, but you did shoot dozens of lions right out in our front yard, although I was never able to see any of them. I wouldn't make fun of Johnny if I were you."

52

Johnny's big blue eyes opened wide as he looked at his mother and brother. "But we really did see some bears. There are lots of them down the street in the woods. And there are natives who live there, just like the Africans, and there are all kinds of poisonous snakes, too."

On and on talked Johnny, to the unbounded amusement of mother and Tom, both of whom knew that these tales were but the product of a vivid, childish imagination and not the downright falsehoods that less understanding people would have called them.

"All right, dear," answered mother. "You may play with Douglas until I call you. Put on your little red sweater. It may be somewhat chilly in the shade of the trees. Have a good time and be sure to come when I call."

"Do you think it's a good idea to let those two little chaps play down there?" questioned Tom, as he picked up his schoolbooks and kissed his mother good-by. "Of course it's only a block away, but there's no telling what mischief they'll get into."

His mother laughed merrily as she began to gather up the breakfast dishes. "Of course they're all right. In fact, I think it's about the safest place that they can go, now that there is so much traffic on the opposite block. Dad and I have been over almost every foot of the small wooded tract, and anyway, there are neighbors on all sides. He and Douglas have been rather badly scratched by the thick undergrowth of bushes and berry vines, but now that they have learned their lesson they are more careful. Run along, or you'll be late. I'll keep an eye on the boys."

But just then the telephone rang noisily and continued ringing at short intervals all morning, for mother, as chairman of a welfare committee, received many calls from reporting club members. In the rush of morning activities the time slipped rapidly by, and still she had not once stepped out onto the porch to call to Johnny or listen for his answer.

Father had just stopped the car on the driveway when they saw Johnny streaking across from Douglas's home. He was pale with excitement and so breathless that he could only stammer his first words.

"Over there. He—he went right—he went—he——"

Mother knelt quickly beside the frightened child and put her arms around him. "There, there, dear," she soothed. "What is it? You can tell mother and Daddy all about it as soon as you catch your breath. You're too excited to talk just yet."

The eyes of the adults met in a knowing look as they took Johnny's hands and led him into the house, where mother sponged off his face and made him sit down in a chair for a few minutes, much against his wishes. But Johnny was too full of his exciting news to remain silent for very long. As soon as he could draw a deep breath he began again.

"I told you this morning that we'd see another bear, and we did, too, Mother. Only he was bigger than any of the others. He was just like this—" and the shining-eyed, excited lad held out his arms as far as they would stretch. "He was the biggest bear I ever saw. He——"

"Where was he, son?" asked father, as he leaned back against the davenport and opened the paper, prepara-tory to reading the daily news.

Then All at Once He Growled Down Deep and Started
Right After Us

"Right out there in the woods, where Douglas and I play all the time. But today we were scared, 'cause this bear growled at us and showed his teeth when we saw him in the bushes. And our bears don't growl at us; they're nice and tame."

Mother smiled down at her youngest as she smoothed his tousled hair. "There, there, honey, let's just forget about it for a few minutes. I'm sure that the natives who live there will capture the animal. Perhaps they will tie him up and keep him for you until tomorrow. I don't want you to go away from home again today. I think you're playing too hard. After your nap perhaps we'll call Doug and have him play in your sandpile with you. Then when brother comes home, you can tell him about the big black bear that you saw."

"But, Mother," Johnny protested, "we didn't just see him. He chased us and chased us. And we yelled and screamed, but nobody paid any attention at all. And then he growled worse than ever, and when he wrinkled back his nose, we saw his long white teeth. They looked so scary. Then all at once he growled down deep, like this—'Gr-r-r woof. Gr-r-r woof!' and started right after us. We ran like everything over back of Douglas's house. But he kept coming along right after us, closer and closer and closer."

Tears filled Johnny's eyes as he swallowed hard. "We were so scared we could hardly get in the garage to shut the door. And even after the door was shut he went round and round outside, growling like this—Gr-r-r! I—I guess I don't want to shut up any more bears in Doug's garage—not ever again."

After the weary, frightened little boy had been tucked in for his afternoon nap, mother and father talked over the matter and decided that he had better play quietly at home for a few days until the excitement of the morning was forgotten.

"He has such a vivid imagination that he'll be a nervous wreck if he's allowed to have all these adventures," father asserted. "Better have Doug's mother keep him at home too, and let both of them quiet down a bit. What one can't think of, the other one does, I imagine."

"That's right. It's too bad to separate the little playmates, but this excursion today has proved to be rather a trying ordeal. So we'll keep him at home for a few days, as you suggested. When Tom gets here he will play with him. He's always so kind to Johnny and does so many nice things to amuse him."

Johnny was awake when Tom arrived, and for a few minutes the conversation concerned only Johnny's thrilling morning adventure. At last mother spoke, hoping to put an end to the torrent of words pouring from her small son's lips.

"Why don't you take Tom over to Doug's garage and show him where the bear went huffing and puffing around the building, Johnny? Then you can come back here and play a game with big brother."

"That'd be fine, Mother," nodded Tom, understanding that his mother wished to end Johnny's excited conversation. "Come along, half-pint, and we'll go exploring, right in our neighbor's yard."

Only a few minutes had elapsed before mother heard pounding feet and cries of "Mother, mother, come here."

As she ran to the front door she almost collided with the hurrying boys.

"He's right. It's true," gasped Tom excitedly. "It really *is* true."

"What's true, dear?" asked mother quickly. "I don't understand what you're talking about. What do you mean?"

"Over there," gulped Tom, looking down in wonder at the small boy clinging fast to him. "For once Johnny wasn't pretending, Mother. There *are* bear tracks over there. Doug's father is measuring them, and he says that they're the biggest he's seen in all his years of hunting."

"There really *is* a big black bear out there in the woods, Mother," shrilled Johnny. "And he almost caught Doug and me, and ate us up. He chased us as fast as anything. I told you and father about it, and you wouldn't even listen."

Mother sank weakly into the nearest chair while Tommy called his father. When father reached home he found armed residents and members of the city, county, and State police forces ready to hunt the animal, which had somehow managed to wander down from the distant mountains into the small woods in this thickly settled area.

The Newspaper Photographer Took a Picture of Johnny in the Spot Where He Had Seen the Bear

The very real bruin was not located until the following morning, when his travels again brought him back to the berry bushes in the wooded tract. And then the snarling, four-hundred-pound animal was shot and shortly afterward removed by the Humane Society employees.

"Well, well, I hear you're quite a bear hunter," laughed the newspaper photographer, as he took a picture of Johnny standing in the very spot where he had first seen the wild animal. "Are you going to be another 'Bring-'Em-Back-Alive Frank Buck?'"

He handed his discarded flash bulbs to the little boy, who had asked if he might have them so that he could play grocery store, adding them to his other "merchandise."

"No, sir," soberly answered the unsmiling Johnny, shivering a little as he looked at the huge bear sprawled lifeless on the ground. "My brother Tom asked me that question too. But I said I'd rather be just plain old 'Stay-Alive Johnny.' No more bears for me!"

CHAPTER 6 *Swift Waters*

GINGER ROLLED over and opened one sleepy eye as she reached out and turned off the alarm. She had just pulled the covers up over her head when her mother spoke.

"None of that, young lady. It's time to get up! Don't you remember that today we decided to set the alarm a half hour earlier than usual so we wouldn't be late? We must be ready in plenty of time, for we may have to wait for a bus."

Virginia (Ginger) and her mother, Mrs. Leach, were spending the summer in Eugene, Oregon, where they were living in a one-room apartment in a large former fraternity home that, because of the housing shortage, had been converted into small apartments. Although it was Saturday and the large building was filled with the familiar bustle of week-day activities and the sound of children's merry voices, Ginger and her mother were not taking part in the usual tasks. For this day was the

Sabbath, and they were planning to attend church services in the large downtown Seventh-day Adventist church.

"I'll get up right now!" cheerily answered the sixteen-year-old girl, as she threw back the bed covers and jumped hastily out on the rug. "I was so sleepy that at first I thought it was time to go to work at the cleaners. I was trying to catch a few extra winks, just as I always did down at Lodi Academy when the rising bell sounded. Then I realized it was Sabbath."

"Well, hurry, dear. I've laid out the clothes that you decided to wear, and although it's August, I don't believe that you'll be too warm if you wear your new gray coat. Or perhaps you'd prefer to carry it over your arm. You'll look very sweet in your new white blouse and gray skirt. I thought you'd want your lace-trimmed slip also, so I put it with your clothing."

She smiled proudly at her pretty daughter as they closed their door and started down the hall. She thought how much she and Virginia were enjoying the summer months spent in the old, vine-covered home right on the green banks of the tree-lined millrace—the small, swift stream whose deep channel cut across the University of Oregon district and on through part of the city. Many happy evenings had been spent in fireplace "sings" with the five or six congenial families who also lived under the big red roof. Ginger had proved to be especially popular with the many small children, who liked to watch her splash and play in the cold stream, which was too deep and too swift for them to enter.

One of the younger girls heard their footsteps and

ran to meet them. It was four-year-old Judy Luck, who loved Ginger dearly. As the older girl bent to kiss the rosy cheek, Judy exclaimed, "Oh, Gingie, you look so pretty with your new black shoes and new hat. I wish I could go with you. Could I, Gingie?"

"O Gingie, You Look So Pretty With Your New Black Shoes and New Hat"

"Not now, honey," laughed Virginia. "We thought we got up quite early, but somehow we must have slowed down, for we've just barely time to have breakfast and get to church. I don't like to be late, and today a visiting minister is speaking, so I want to be sure and hear his sermon. Some other time we'll take you and Dianne to the Sabbath school kindergarten, for they have many interesting stories and songs for little boys and girls."

"Judy, where are you?" a voice called, as Mrs. Luck came up the stairway, hairbrush in hand. "Don't look so worried, Virginia. I'm not going to spank Judy; I'm just going to brush her hair. Blonde hair seems to tangle so quickly. I had to run down to the back porch to see where Dianne was playing. She's the most fearless six-year-old I ever saw. Every day I must remind her to stay away from the water's edge. It's swift even for a good swimmer

With a Quick, Clean-cut Dive She Flashed Into the Water

like you. It makes me shudder to think what would happen if a child fell in."

Virginia waved good-by to Judy as she and her mother hurried downstairs to the big community kitchen where each family prepared meals. Four women were already there, and for a few minutes everyone visited in the cheerful breakfast room. Then one of the women stepped out onto the porch for a minute but returned almost instantly. "Quick—quick. Help her! She's out there——" she gasped, almost too frightened to speak.

"Why, what's happened!" exclaimed Virginia, as she ran to the woman's side. "Who is out there? You are as white as a sheet! Here, sit down in this chair. I'll get you a glass of water."

"No—no," the frightened woman gasped as she pushed Virginia away. "You don't understand. Don't stop. It—it's Dianne. One of the little boys in the yard called to me. He—he said that Dianne had fallen in the millrace. Hurry!"

Quickly Virginia and her mother ran outside, with all the others following. Virginia knew that she was the only one present who could swim, and without stopping to realize her own possible danger she ran swiftly to the millrace bank.

"Wait, Ginger," her mother called. "Take off your skirt. It'll hold you back. Take it off."

Virginia paused only long enough to unfasten her waistband and step out of her gray suit skirt. Then, catching a glimpse of the drowning child, with a quick, clean-cut dive she flashed into the swift water. But just at that moment the little figure sank out of sight. The frightened onlookers wondered frantically where little Dianne could be, when all at once Mrs. Leach cried out, "Look! There she is—over by the other bank. Oh! but she is drifting away so fast that Gingie will miss her! It's too late. Too late!"

Through tear-filled eyes they stared at the small, blue-clad figure, now drifting motionlessly away, feet first and arms outspread. They watched in frozen horror as Virginia reached the opposite bank only long enough to catch her breath. Then, as she once again caught sight of Dianne, she gave a little spring that sent her flying into the water—and momentarily she disappeared.

Mrs. Leach wondered desperately whether the mill-race would claim two victims that August day. She felt so weak and helpless that she almost fainted from terror and despair.

"If only I could do something," she thought wildly. "If only I could help my precious girl and that little child!" And then her answer came as clearly as though a voice had spoken in her ear.

"Pray!"

Pray? Why, of course. The words rang in her ears: "When thou passest through the waters, I will be with thee. . . . Fear not: for I am with thee."

Eyes fixed on the unbroken water, she prayed as she had never prayed before in her life. She knew that Gingie, somewhere in that deep channel, was even then praying to the One who had said, "If thou canst believe, all things are possible to him that believeth."

And then, four feet beyond the now barely visible Dianne, Virginia's head broke the surface of the waves.

But even then, because of the motion of the water, she did not see the little child. Mrs. Leach's lips moved silently as she stared unwinkingly toward Virginia; her fingernails pressed deep into her palms.

"There, Gingie," she kept repeating within herself. "Dianne's right there. She's near you. Oh! can't you see her—just below the surface. Look, my child. Look!"

At that very instant Dianne's little face and hands came to the surface for only a second, but that was sufficient time for Virginia to reach out in a mad lunge and grasp a handful of long blonde hair.

Next came the struggle to reach shore and the outstretched hands of the two little boys who were the only ones on that side of the stream. Dianne's little playmates dragged her up on the bank, where she lay, still and cold. The almost exhausted rescuer pulled herself up on the edge of the stream and then hurried to the three little figures dreading lest she had reached the tiny girl too late.

She ran to Dianne and turned her over on her stomach in order to give artificial respiration. But before that could be started, Dianne gasped for air, opened her eyes, and started crying. Oh, what pitiful crying! But how glad Virginia was to hear the sound. She gathered the little drenched, frightened child up in her arms and held her tight, murmuring soothing words until the women had time to run around by way of the bridge and reach them.

One of the women carried Dianne into the house, where many willing hands cared for her and for her frightened mother, who had known nothing about the near tragedy until her half-drowned child was brought into the house.

"Are you all right, dear?" Mrs. Leach asked Virginia as they sat on the bank, resting for a few moments.

"Yes, Mother, I'm all right," Virginia replied quietly. Everything seemed very peaceful and calm after the few moments of violent stress. Then the girl spoke again as she stared into the silently moving waters, and watched the little black hat with the now-wilted veil become a speck far down the stream.

"Mother, I could never have done it alone!"

Mrs. Leach nodded. She knew well what her daughter meant. Many times she had seen her play in the mill-race, but never before had she been able to go so nearly straight across that swift current. Yet with His help she had just done that very thing!

When they were once again in their room, Virginia said, "Mother, please don't tell anyone about this, will you? After all, it was no more than anyone else would have done. And I don't want people making a fuss over me!"

But in this respect her wish was not to be granted. Her picture and the story of the daring rescue appeared not only in the local paper, which carried a front-page feature story, with the statement that she was being recommended for the Carnegie Medal, but also in newspapers throughout the United States from the San Francisco *Examiner* to the New York *Times*. Several news commentators mentioned the rescue on their radio programs, and Virginia received many letters of commendation.

However, the unsought recognition which she prized the most came on Tuesday evening, August 14. Just three days after the accident, as she and her mother sat in the Eugene Hotel dining room with the Luck family, Mr. and Mrs. Luck presented her with a beautiful little rose gold wrist watch. The dinner was delicious, and everyone had a wonderful time. But best of all were the words of little Dianne and Judy, who looked at her with love and devotion shining in their eyes as they said, "We'll always love you, Ginger."

Oh, how thankful Virginia was, as she looked at little Dianne, for God's help and sustaining power.

"Yes," she thought, "it's a wonderful feeling—that of having served others. But it is even more wonderful to feel God's helping hand and to know that your prayers are being answered."

CHAPTER 7

The Strength
of an Ox

THE COLD wind slashed across Jed's face as he hastily climbed into the borrowed cart out in front of the old log cabin. Pulling the bearskin robe up to his chin, he watched his father carry in the last armload of wood, latch the door, and hurry across the frozen ground toward him.

"Br-r-r! I'm cold," Jed said through chattering teeth. Already his nose was reddened by the frosty autumn air.

"I know you are, son," said his father. "It's a bitter day for certain, but I couldn't go without replacing the same amount of firewood as we'd used. That's the unwritten law of the trail, you know. Some poor fellow in need of warmth might come stumbling along to this same deserted cabin. Perhaps he'd be so cold that he couldn't cut wood. That very thing happened to a mail carrier near my boyhood home."

Jethro Wheeler sprang into the cart, picked up the reins, and called, "Let's go, Buck," and the old ox moved slowly but steadily forward, head down against the rising wind.

"What happened then, Father?" questioned Jed in a small voice. He waited, and after a few minutes again asked, "But what happened to the mail carrier? Couldn't he find the cabin?"

"Eh?" asked Mr. Wheeler. He turned his startled gaze upon his young son. "Oh, I'm sorry. I was watching old Buck—I don't like the way he's breathing—and I forgot all about my story.

"Well, this mail carrier had crossed the mountains many times, traveling on snowshoes. He had always made the long trip in safety, for he stopped overnight at a certain cabin shelter that he kept supplied with kindling and wood. But on this particular trip he was caught in a severe, unexpected blizzard. Hours behind schedule, he managed to stumble through the unlatched cabin door, and fell half-frozen upon the dirt floor. It was all he could do to drag himself to his knees and crawl to the fireplace where he kept the moss and kindling in readiness. But when he got there——"

"O Father," broke in Jed, "could he light the fire? Or——"

"No, son, he couldn't," Mr. Wheeler soberly replied. "For some unknown traveler had stayed overnight in the shelter, used up the wood and kindling, and left without bringing in a fresh supply. No, the poor man could have lighted a fire, but he wasn't able to go out and cut wood. It was a week before a rescue party broke trail and found him, and long before that he had frozen to death.

"But here! All this happened many years ago. I think

that we've had enough talk about freezing; we'll have ourselves chilled to the bone if we aren't careful. Pull your ear flaps down and be sure to keep your red wool muffler up around your throat. Mother will be heartsick if you become ill again."

Jethro Wheeler glanced worriedly down at the small, huddled figure leaning against him. It had been a long, hard trip out to the nearest settlement, with the two slow oxen pulling the heavy wagon. Not even the necessity of getting much-needed supplies would have forced him to undertake the journey at this time of year, with its threat of sudden blizzards. He had made one trip early in the fall, and they could have managed until spring if necessary, although they might have had short rations before the arrival of good weather. However, little Jed, their only child, had not been well for some time. Frequently he lay in his rude bunk for days at a time, his face burning with fever, his choked voice calling for a cool drink. At last his mother, frantic with worry, had insisted that the child be taken to the nearest doctor, five days' journey by ox team.

"Well," thought Jethro grimly, "I took the boy to the doctor all right, and he gave us some medicine and some good advice that's not going to be of much help unless we soon reach shelter." His sober gaze stared straight ahead, over the broad, slowly moving back of old Buck, and he frowned worriedly as he recalled the physician's final warning before they left Little Rock settlement.

"I'm sure that the boy will be all right if you follow the treatment outlined and give him the medicine twice a day. But don't let him get chilled, whatever you do. In

Infantry Warriors Charged Wood in Dress at the Small Stream Leaving Ancient Ville

his weakened condition it might prove fatal. He's not strong enough to stand real blizzard weather, so be sure to keep him in where it's warm."

"Keep him in where it's warm!" Mr. Wheeler thought grimly. Already the wind had sharpened. It moaned a wild, weird song as it blew across the frozen land. A fierce gust caught Buck full face, and the tired, patient creature wavered and turned toward the left.

"Back Gee, Buck. Back Gee [come to the right], I say," he called, and sat tensely until the plodding animal again struggled forward straight into the face of the rising gale.

"Poor Buck. He misses Charley. I'm sure he does," said Jed through chattering teeth.

"Yes, son, I'm sure he does," his father nodded. "It's natural that he would. I've had them both from the time they were little calves, long before you were born." He glanced down at the child and then continued talking, more for the purpose of keeping Jed awake than anything else, for the slashing wind made talking difficult. Every sentence made him sharply draw his breath.

"Yes, I began yoking them together. Then, when they were yearlings, I branded them with our own Lazy C mark. After that I had them drag logs around the field for practice in pulling. I didn't use any harness—just a yoke and bow around the neck, and the yoke fastened to the wagon tongue by log chains. They were so well trained that they'd work together or each would work singly when fastened to a small plow. It's a good thing for us that Buck was taught to work alone. Otherwise he wouldn't pull this cart."

"And you even trained Buck and Charley so that you could ride them!" Jed added, with a small boy's admiration for his father.

"That's right. I did. They've been a mighty fine pair of oxen. They've always been so gentle that I've never had to cut off their horns. I've always given them good care and fed them well on hay, corn shucks, and ear corn.

"But now they're really too old to work. I wouldn't have driven them on this trip if I'd had time to go over to Mr. Long's and pay him the $75 he's asking for his yoke of steers. But as soon as we get home I'll not work Buck any more."

"Oh, how I wish we had our big wagon with Buck and Charley pulling it together," Jed burst forth. "Why did Charley have to hurt his leg? If he hadn't stepped in that gopher hole we'd have had all our provisions with us. We could have stayed at that old cabin and waited for the storm to blow over, for we'd have plenty of food. Now you'll have to go all the way back to Halfway House to get him and our wagon load of winter supplies!"

Round and round creaked the rickety wheels. On and on plodded the weary ox. Lower and lower sank Jethro Wheeler's heart as he bent his snow-whitened head to look at his child.

"We must go forward. We *must!* If we don't reach home tonight, it will be too late. It's getting colder and colder every minute."

Just then Buck plunged to one side and started to back track on the trail.

"Whoa come, Buck. Whoa come [come to the left]," he shouted. For once the ox did not respond to his master's voice, but stood still, head hanging low and tail turned toward the tempest.

"Let's go. Come on, Buck. Let's go [get up]," Jethro Wheeler called out. "Come on, Buck. Only a few more miles, and we'll be home. Try once more." He sprang from the cart and hurried to the side of the ox.

"What's wrong, old fellow?" he called. "I've been worried about you. What's wrong?" But even as he put his mittened hand upon the neck of the faithful beast he started back in dismay. For at that very instant Buck, worn out by his fierce exertion, dropped heavily to the snowy ground and lay there, lifeless.

"Dead. Buck's dead," Jethro Wheeler thought frantically. "What shall I do? What *can* I do!"

To attempt to carry the boy the remaining distance would be fatal, both for himself and for his child. He knew that he had not sufficient strength to carry even the lightest burden in the face of the howling gale. And it was unthinkable to expose Jed any further to the biting zero weather. Unless he could be kept warm until rescued he would surely die.

Jed's father beat his hands together as he walked around and around the sled. A dozen wild schemes flashed through his mind, only to be rejected as impractical.

"But what shall I do to save my boy? I *must* save my son."

Half-blinded by the snow and sleet, he stumbled across the still body of old Buck. And at that instant he had his answer. But could he do this thing? Would this last desperate effort save the life of his child?

For a moment he stood still, dreading the decision. Then, grim-faced, he reached into the cart, pulled out his sharp hunting knife, and set to work to open the body of the lifeless ox.

"What—what is it, Father?" whispered Jed, as he half roused to feel himself being lifted from the seat. But almost instantly his eyelids fluttered shut, and he re-sumed his heavy breathing.

"Listen, Jed. Listen to me," his father called des-perately, shaking Jed awake. "Jed, listen to me."

"Y-es, Father? What-what is it? I'm—so sleepy. Are we home? Wh-where's mother?"

"Son, I'm going home—now—to mother. I'll come back as soon as I can get help. I can't carry you in this storm. Are you listening? Listen carefully, Jed. I'm leav-ing you here. Do you understand? You're to stay here!"

Now the heavy eyelids flew wide open as Jed roused and gasped, "Here? In the cold? Why, I—I'll freeze. Take me with you, Father. I'll walk. I'm sure I can walk. Only don't leave me. Please don't leave me, Father."

Never again in Jed's lifetime was he so frightened as he was at that moment, when he realized what his father had just told him. What could his father mean. He stared wildly at him.

"Listen carefully, Jed," his father repeated. "I'm going to roll you up in this robe—just like this. There. Now I'm going to leave you while I go for help, but you're not going to be cold. You're going to be in a safe, warm place. You must stay there until I return. Don't try to move. Remember, you must stay there until I come back for you. If you do as I say, you will be quite safe."

Without trusting himself to say another word he swiftly lifted Jed and carried him over to the spot where the body of old Buck lay, lifeless but warm. And then Jed understood. His father stooped and carefully placed his son inside the opened body of the ox, turning him so that he could breathe fresh air and yet covering him so that he was protected from the storm.

The old settlers still tell of that terrible early blizzard and of the almost superhuman struggle of Jethro Wheeler to reach his home. And it was the talk of the entire countryside after the rescue party retraced his steps over the weary miles to the place where he had been forced to leave his son. For there, inside the snow-covered animal, exactly as he had left him long hours before, lay Jed, safe and warm. There he lay, opening his eyes to look up into his father's eager face—saved by the strength of an ox.

Inside the Snow-covered Body of the Ox Lay
Little Jed, Safe and Warm

CHAPTER 8

Flashing Fangs

AS HAROLD entered the barber shop he stopped short in stunned surprise.

"Why, hello, Mr. Hibbard," he stammered, staring first at the shiny metal wheel chair and then at the happy face of its invalid occupant.

"Well, I'm certainly surprised to see you downtown," he hurriedly added. "But it's wonderful that you can get out this way. And your chair—when did you get it? And where——"

"Here, here," laughed George Hibbard, as he bent his head forward so that the barber could run the clippers over his strong, sunburned neck. "Not so fast, my young friend. I'll gladly answer your questions, but first I'm going to ask a few. Aren't you getting to be a regular summer visitor in Burns? Let me see; isn't this your third summer in eastern Oregon? Why, I believe that you really like our little town of Burns."

"Oh, I do," stoutly agreed Harold. "I like the boys

and girls and the people—they're so friendly. And I especially like you, Mr. Hibbard. You're always so pleasant and so much fun that I never think about your
being paral——Well, I mean——" His voice trailed off
as he stopped in confusion.

"That's quite all right, Harold. You needn't be em-
barrassed because you mentioned my paralyzed condition. Soon after my accident a number of years ago I
made up my mind that if I lived I would never let people
feel that I was essentially any different from anyone else.
I've been fortunate, too, for though I am paralyzed from
my neck down I still have full control of my voice, my
hearing, and my eyesight. Thus there are many things
that I can enjoy.

"But here, if you have time for a visit now, perhaps
you'd like to push my chair up the hill to my home. I'll
show you the motto of a famous group of people who
are handicapped in everything but bravery of spirit, and
then we'll talk awhile. I'll leave word here for Gene, my
nephew, as he was coming back soon to take me home."

George Hibbard served as a rental librarian for the
little Oregon city. As they entered his large, book-filled
library bedroom, which overlooked the vast expanse of
Harney Valley, he nodded his head toward a hand-
lettered motto that hung near his bed.

"Read it aloud if you care to, Harold," he said
quietly. "It has been a constant inspiration to me, as I
am sure that it has been to countless others."

"Never Martyrdom shall I seek;
Never Sarcasm shall I speak;
Never Ingratitude shall I show;

Never Discontented shall I grow;
Never Sympathy shall I desire;
Never Self-pity shall I acquire.

"Never Unhappiness shall I spread;
Never Tears of Remorse shall I shed;
Never Sorrow shall I sing;
Never to Selfishness shall I cling;
Never Criticism shall I write;
Never of God shall I lose sight."

Harold's voice stopped, and he drew a deep breath before he again spoke. "Why, that's a wonderful poem," he volunteered soberly. "And you're just like that, too, Mr. Hibbard."

"Thank you, Harold, I'm afraid I'm not like that, although I try to be," the librarian said quietly. "But here. Do you remember the long, rubber-tipped stick which I hold in my mouth when reading and with which I turn the pages of the book or magazine? Yes, I see that you do. Then you'll be interested in knowing that I've found a further use for that trusty stick and for my good strong teeth. Can you guess what it is?"

"Another use?" Puzzled, the youthful visitor wrinkled his forehead and shook his head. "N-n-no, I can't imagine."

"Well, quite soon I expect to have my new electric typewriter, and as soon as it comes I'll invite you over to watch me use it," stated George.

"Use a typewriter!" gasped Harold, sitting suddenly forward on his chair. "But—but how, when you can't move your arms at all, and——"

"Didn't I tell you that I'd found a further use for my trusty stick?" queried George, laughing heartily at Harold's amazement.

"You mean you type with *that?*" the boy blurted out.

"Correct! While visiting my sisters in Portland last summer I had an opportunity to use a borrowed electric typewriter. I sat up in my new wheel chair, held this rubber-tipped stick in my mouth, lightly touched it to the keys, and wrote for six hours the first day. When I finished I was exhausted, but happier by far than I had been for years."

"Why, that's wonderful!" exclaimed Harold. "But how did you ever get the idea of trying to do this? I'd never have known enough to even try."

"A friend of mine who had attended a writers' conference told me that there she had met an extremely talented crippled girl who had the use of just one finger for typing. She said that she was sure that I could do as well, and to my surprise I found that I really could type on one of these easily operated new machines. Certainly I shall be very happy when I own one."

"Are you going to write any stories, Mr. Hibbard?" eagerly questioned Harold. "Last summer you said that you'd like to put down on paper some of your experiences. I think that the stories you've told me would make exciting reading for any boy or girl. I've never forgotten 'King and Queen Go Hunting,' or the snake story, 'Double Death.' I've told them ever so many times."

"Yes, Harold, that's just what I hope to do," nodded George. "I don't know about stories, but I'm going to try some nature articles. Whatever I write will be true, how-

6

ever, for I don't care to waste my time writing fiction. There are too many wonderful wildlife stories just waiting to be told."

"I know that," solemnly agreed the visitor. "Do you remember that when I first met you I didn't know anything about the out-of-doors? Then you began telling me stories about snakes and deer and coyotes and—— Why, that reminds me! In school last term our teacher read us a story about Louis Pasteur and his discovery of a cure for hydrophobia. Right away I thought about you, and wondered if you'd ever seen a mad dog or a mad coyote. None of us had—not even our teacher."

"Yes, Harold, as a matter of fact, I have," said George rather soberly. "And it is a fearful sight—one that I would not care to see again. Would you like to hear the story?"

"Oh, indeed I would," eagerly assented Harold, drawing his chair as close as possible to George's wheel chair. "Please tell me."

"Well, this happened a number of years ago, long before you were born. It was late in the fall. In fact, it lacked only a few weeks of being Christmas when that dreadful disease influenza began to strike down members of almost every Burns family.

"Today we speak of it as the flu. And today the patient calls his doctor, obtains one of the new miracle drugs, and recovers rapidly. But soon after World War I, when people in the United States first experienced a real influenza epidemic, to be ill with this disease was a matter of life or death. Many people died, for there were no miracle drugs then, and nurses were scarce. Mother became very much alarmed, and insisted that she be allowed to take all of us children out of town to our small mountain cabin.

" 'You'll have to stay here so that you can see as many of your dental patients as possible,' she told my father, 'and Roberta had better stay to cook for you. Every few days you can bring necessary supplies up as far as the pasture gate, and in that way we'll manage all right. I dare not expose the children to this epidemic. Several of them have had colds all fall and the influenza might prove fatal. I'm sure that it is best for us to go to the mountains.'

"After much discussion my father reluctantly agreed to this plan, and within a few days we had moved some miles out of town, up in the foothills of the Blue Mountains.

"By now the weather had turned very cold, and the older boys were kept busy chopping down small trees near the cabin, sawing and cutting them into stovewood lengths, and piling them in neat stacks against the outer cabin walls. Mother was determined to prepare for a real siege, if need be."

"Did you cut down any of the trees?" questioned Harold.

"Oh, no. I was very small then, but I felt that I was really doing most of the work when I went out and filled the chip basket with the fragments of wood and bark, which we used for kindling. You see, this was before our present days of automatic furnace heat and electric or gas ranges.

"It was also before the time of kitchen sinks and hot

and cold running water in the average home. We had the running water all right, but it was in an icy mountain creek several hundred yards away. I usually felt it my duty to go with the girls when they took the water buckets down to the willow-bordered stream to fill them and carry them back to the kitchen. Sometimes we had to crack the ice in order to dip those buckets into the creek."

"Br-r-r! That must have been cold work," broke in Harold. "It makes my teeth chatter just to think about it. All that work to get water! I guess I've never appreciated our water faucets as much as I should."

"You probably haven't," nodded the librarian. "We often don't appreciate the many conveniences that we now have until we realize that people lived—and many still do—without them.

"But I must hurry on with my story. I neglected to tell you that we took our young dog along with us when we left Burns. I guess that I was really responsible for including him in the family group. He was a fine sheep dog, and I had claimed him for my very own. During our waking hours we were inseparable, as we were during our sleeping hours, for nothing would do but that Shep must sleep on a clean gunny sack at the foot of my bed.

"Although at that time I was the baby of the family, mother never seemed the least bit nervous about having me outside, for Shep watched me with an eagle eye. And no small wild creature or stranger ever approached me without Shep barking a warning that all could hear.

"On this particular day dad had come up as far as the pasture gate and had brought food and other provisions for us, as well as local news of interest to mother. She had gone down to meet and talk with him, for he did not want to come near us children, thinking that from contact with his patients he might carry upon him the dread influenza germs. I can remember that she looked very sober-faced as she returned to the cabin, calling to the older boys to carry up the supplies and put them in the kitchen. But it was not until evening that she told us this news.

" 'Children,' she said, as we stood around the glowing, pot-bellied stove, 'your father told me that another terrible disease has broken out in Harney County.' "

"But what *could* be worse?" anxiously asked the young listener. "Didn't you say that the influenza epidemic killed a number of people?"

"Yes, Harold, it did," nodded George, "but this other disease was the dreaded and terrible one that until a few years ago doomed its hundreds of victims to a certain, horrible end. This disease was called rabies, or hydrophobia."

"Oo-h!" exclaimed the boy. "Now I understand. And it wasn't until Louis Pasteur found a serum for the bite of a mad animal that anyone attacked could hope to be saved. What an awful thing that must have been—to have had no hope of a cure."

"That is the very thing my mother mentioned that evening as she told us my father's message. She warned us to be very careful to stay near the house. She told us we must not wander outside the fence except on necessary errands, and in that case the older boys would go armed. Dad had told her that many rabid coyotes were

Straight Toward Me It Came, Red Eyes Gleaming, Hanging Jaws
Covered With Froth

running rampant through the fields and mountains, biting anything unfortunate enough to cross their paths. One of dad's friends had narrowly escaped a sudden attack by his prize bull, which had suddenly gone mad.

"Well, for a few days I was afraid to go outdoors. We kept Shep cooped up inside with us, too, but at last the dog became so restless that we mustered up enough courage to go out near the back porch. Nothing occurred to frighten any of us, and as we saw no signs of any wild animals near the ranch, we gradually became bolder and bolder. It was not long before I completely forgot about any possible danger.

"On this particular early evening I had gone to the creek with Eugenia and Hazel, but when they started back to the house with the heavy, dripping water bucket sagging between them, I stayed by the water's edge. Shep had spied a big gray jack rabbit and had started off in fast pursuit. By the time I had called and whistled him back to my side the girls had entered the house, so I decided to wander just a few steps farther along the creek bank.

"We walked farther than I had intended, when suddenly a low growl from Shep abruptly halted me.

" 'What is it, boy?' I called. 'Come on, Shep. That rabbit's far away over the hills by this time. Stop your growling and come along.' Another louder growl from Shep was my answer. I looked intently at him and felt my heart beat faster as I noticed his stiff-legged pose and saw him bare his long white teeth. His brown eyes glared fiercely toward the woods which crowded down close to our small barn, and the hairs on the back of his neck fairly bristled.

" 'Come on, old boy. Come here,' I again commanded. But Shep paid no attention to me.

"A sound caught my ears and I stopped dead still as the crashing noise of breaking bushes and tree branches echoed and re-echoed through the hills. Nearer and nearer it came, and Shep's growls increased in fierce- ness and in volume.

" 'What can it be?' I thought desperately. 'A hungry bear? A cougar?' Even then the true explanation did not occur to me until all at once a rough, gray-furred animal staggered out of the willows. It bumped blindly against first one tree and then another, but still plunged onward in its mad flight. Straight toward me it came, red eyes gleaming, hanging jaws covered with froth.

"I was absolutely frozen with fear. For the moment I couldn't have moved if my life had depended upon it. I stood there for what seemed an eternity, while larger and larger loomed the rabid animal. And then, just as Shep leaped forward, I heard my mother scream.

" 'Run, George. Run for your life.'

"Her piercing cry broke through my spellbound fright so that just as Shep sprang at the raging coyote I turned and fled, sobbing with fright.

"Though I ran faster and faster, the cabin seemed to move farther and farther away, until I despaired of ever reaching its safety. But reach home I did, to collapse into my mother's waiting arms. Quickly she pulled me inside and bolted the door.

"Mother and all of us children huddled together while the fight raged outside. It was dreadful to listen to the snarls and growls of the brave dog and the mad coyote, and to feel the thud of their bodies as, time after time, they crashed against the cabin walls.

"At last it was all over. Now the only sound outside was the rippling of the swift mountain stream as it rushed downhill and the faint, faraway eerie bark of a distant coyote.

" 'I'm going out, Mother. I'm going out there to get Shep,' I wailed, as I raised my swollen, tear-stained face from mother's lap.

" 'Wait, dear,' she counseled. 'Wait awhile until we're sure it's safe to go.'

"To the loud tick-tock of the old clock the minutes dragged slowly by. At last mother rose and crossed the room to the kitchen door. She reached up to the deerhorn wall rack and took down dad's old gun.

" 'I want all of you to stay in this room,' she said. 'Yes, you older children as well. I'm going to step out on the porch and look for Shep, but none of you are to come unless I call for you. Do you understand?'

"The older children nodded solemnly and I choked out a tearful 'Yes, Mother,' for I was just a small boy, and Shep was my dearest treasure.

"It seemed as though a long, long time passed by, but I suppose that in reality it was but a moment or so. And then—we heard a shot. Just one shot! I screamed and clutched Eugenia, while the boys, forgetful of mother's orders, ran outside."

"What—what had happened?" stammered Harold breathlessly.

"A very wonderful and heart-touching thing had oc-curred," gravely answered George. "When mother

stepped out onto the back porch, the gun aimed at whatever danger might be in her way, she saw a sight that
brought tears to her eyes. There, near the back steps,
mangled and dead, lay the body of the mad coyote, and
halfway up the stairway, where he had crawled in his
frantic desire to reach us, lay poor Shep, unconscious
and bleeding.

"Mother has often said that she had never performed
any harder task than that which she had to do at that
time. Taking careful aim, she———"

"Shot Shep? Your mother shot the dog that had saved
your life? Oh, how could she! That was cruel," exclaimed
Harold, with tears in his own eyes.

"I know how you feel, Harold," nodded George, "for
I was heartbroken when she told me. It was a long time
before I really recovered from my grief, but now I understand that what mother did was the kindest service that
she could have performed for Shep. He was so badly
injured that he could not have lived, and even if he had
lived, he would have developed hydrophobia, for the
coyote was mad."

"But couldn't Shep have been given the Pasteur treatment? Couldn't something have been done for him?" protested Harold.

"You must remember that we were miles from town,
without telephone service and without transportation.
And then it was a long and expensive journey from Burns
to a large city where such a treatment at that time might
have been available. There were a number of good rea-
sons why mother's brave action was the only logical one,
hard though it seemed to us then.

"But Shep had a funeral—what we called a military funeral—for we fired a gun salute over his grave. Then we made a wooden tombstone and carved his name deeply upon it. The weather-beaten letters are there to this day:

SHEP
A BRAVE DOG
HE DIED TO SAVE OTHERS

"After this event we did not remain very long at the cabin, for mother was afraid that other rabid animals might come near. As soon as dad made his next trip up to see us, we returned to town with him. Before we left, I cried again over Shep's grave and vowed that I would never forget him. And I never have, for he was in truth a noble creature and one who gladly laid down his life for his friends.

"But, there, Harold, I'm afraid this story has been a sad one, and I don't want you to think that all our summer visits will bring tears to your eyes. Come over again soon, and I'll tell you about the nest of gold that Eugenia found in the rimrock."

"I surely will, Mr. Hibbard. And while your other stories may be more cheerful than this one, they surely can't be any more thrilling," said Harold. "My school friends will certainly sit up and take notice when I tell them your story of the 'Flashing Fangs.' "

He Cautiously Crept Up on a Large Rock, Where He Lay Flat,
Looking Out Through His Field Glasses

CHAPTER 9

Desert
Capture

"COME IN, Harold," called George Hibbard, as Harold knocked at the half-opened door. "I was just hoping that you'd come over this morning. I want you to meet Margaret Ann Williamson, and then you can listen to the story that I've promised to tell her. Margaret Ann's mother lived here in Burns when she was a little girl. She used to spend a great deal of time right here in our yard, playing with my brothers and sisters. Now Margaret Ann is visiting her cousin, Sally Donegan. She's been begging me for an animal story, so now that you're here I'll have an audience of two listeners."

Harold smiled at the little blue-eyed girl who sat so primly in the leather chair by the librarian's bed, and she smiled shyly in return.

"What's the story today, Mr. Hibbard?" the boy questioned eagerly. "I do hope it's about the nest of gold that you mentioned last time. I've been looking forward to hearing that one ever since then. It sounds quite mysterious."

"No, we'll wait until next time for the story of the nest. Margaret Ann's especially interested in horses, and so I'm going to tell her about an animal that can outrun the swiftest horse. In fact, it can outdistance most land animals, even when painfully wounded. It has been known to travel sixty miles an hour."

"Then it must be a coyote," broke in Margaret Ann, her eyes glistening with excitement. "We saw one out on the desert between here and Bend."

"No, it isn't a coyote," answered George, shaking his head. "This animal is the American pronghorn antelope, which is found only in North America. Before I tell you the story, which I first heard from my father, I'll tell you young people a little about the antelope.

"Many years ago there were millions of antelopes in the West, where they, like the buffalo, provided food for the Indians. Then, as the white man began to hunt with guns, these huge herds were almost wiped out. In addition, many of those surviving fell prey to a cattle disease called fossy-jaw. Finally, about 1900, only a few of these interesting animals remained, and they were found only in the most isolated parts of the country.

"About 1910 various wildlife enthusiasts laid plans to preserve this game animal. In 1924 there were less than 26,000 of them left in the United States, but since then refuges have been established by the Government in Nevada, Wyoming, and Oregon, and in 1937 the number had increased to 130,000."

"Did you say that there was an antelope refuge in Oregon?" inquired Harold. "I've never heard that before. Where is it, or do you know?"

"Indeed I do," smiled George. "The Hart Mountain Antelope Refuge is located in near-by Lake County, in the midst of strange mountains formed of dark, volcanic rock. There the protected animals have increased from only 200 to many thousands. Perhaps someday you can go there, for it is a very interesting place.

"But I must hurry on with my story. It is in May or early June that the female gives birth to two or three fawns. The mother cunningly hides them for the first two days, but by the end of that short time the fawns are swift runners, and within a month they are able to equal the speed of their parents. In fact, it is this speed which often saves the animal from death, although if necessary a mother will turn and fight with her sharp hoofs to defend her fawns.

"Some years ago my father started for the mountains for the express purpose of trying to find and capture a young antelope. As a member of the game commission he felt it necessary to know as much about wildlife as possible. Since it is almost impossible to get near the antelope in his natural surroundings, it was dad's intention to bring a young animal here, where it could live in safety in the enclosed pasture adjoining our place, and from which location he could easily study and observe its actions.

"When dad reached a small, rimrock-enclosed valley he tied his horse behind a tree and then cautiously crept up on a large rock, where he lay flat, looking out through his field glasses."

"Oh, what did he see?" breathed Margaret Ann, holding her hands tightly together.

"What do you think he saw, Harold?" smiled George,

looking from one interested young face to the other.

"An antelope?" replied Harold.

"Yes, he saw an old mother antelope running nervously about whenever any moving thing came into the valley, which she considered her special property. Even swooping eagles and preying hawks were driven away as she charged at them. In addition to this, dad saw the flaring white rosette, formed by the white hairs on the animal's rump. These hairs are raised whenever the animal is alarmed, and they show up plainly even though its tan coat cannot be seen among the sagebrush and rocks.

"Dad knew then that the fawns must be somewhere in that little valley. He knew, also, that if he could only wait patiently he might be lucky enough to see them, for the antelope mother nurses her young ones every two hours. She will feed near them, and then when it is time for them to nurse, she will go toward their hiding place and give some kind of signal."

"What does she do, Mr. Hibbard?" broke in Harold, quite forgetting his accustomed politeness in his interest in the story. "Does she call out?"

"No one has ever been able to learn what signal is given," replied George, "but the young ones come out at once from their hiding place, nurse for about five minutes, and walk about at the mother's heels for exercise. Then the mother antelope, without turning her head or making any audible sound, gives the same mysterious signal. The fawns turn at right angles and go off about 50 or 75 steps into the sage brush, where they hide themselves so well that if you were to pass within several feet of them you probably would not see them."

"Did your father get to see the little babies?" burst forth Margaret Ann, eager to know the answer right away.

"Dad said that he lay on that hard rock for twelve long hours, from six o'clock in the morning to six o'clock at night, but not once did he see that mother nurse her little ones. He didn't know whether she sensed his presence there or what had happened, but he was sure there was some unusual reason for her apparent neglect.

"And then, late in the afternoon, just when dad was about ready to give up and start for home, he saw the mother swerve near a juniper tree. Just as she reached it, a large bobcat jumped down from the branches and ran full speed for the safety of the rimrock some distance away.

"Dad was astonished to see the mother antelope leap in pursuit of the fleeing bobcat. Because of her great speed she soon caught up with the killer. With one bound she struck him with her shoulder, sending the bobcat sprawling into the near-by brush. Hurriedly he struggled to his feet and again started running for safety. Again she struck him with her shoulder, and again he

Dad Was Astonished to See the Mother Antelope Leap in
Pursuit of the Fleeing Bobcat

sprawled flat upon the ground. This happened several times, but at last the frightened bobcat reached the rim-rock and disappeared from sight. I imagine that had he not jumped hastily to his feet each time, she would have trampled him to death beneath her sharp hoofs."

"And did your father get to see the baby fawns?" asked Margaret Ann, cheeks red with excitement. "Oh, I hope he did."

"Yes," nodded George, "he really saw the babies, for after the treed bobcat left the little valley, the mother became less and less nervous. Finally her fluff went down, and soon she gave the signal for the little ones to come out of hiding and nurse. How hungry those poor babies must have been all day, but not once had they dared to show their little noses without hearing their mother's command to come out from hiding.

"Dad carefully marked the spot where they went into hiding, and after the mother had wandered some distance away, he ran down the slope into the valley, cornered one of the fawns, and brought it home, where it became a family pet."

"Oh, it seems cruel to take away her fawn," exclaimed Harold, "especially when she was so brave and had worked so hard to save the little fellows from the bobcat."

"It might seem that way," agreed George, "unless you remember why dad wanted to capture a small antelope. The mother still had her other babies, and dad had the young animal, which he could observe and study. Fluffy never lacked for care and attention, you may be sure.

"You would have laughed if you could have seen him with his foster mother, Nanny, one of our best milk goats. They became very good friends, although when Fluffy was only four months old he was as large as Nanny. Fluffy had the run of the place and would even frolic along near-by streets, much to the delight of all the neighborhood children. But when mealtime rolled around, he was right back here with Nanny, and whenever dad came home, the little fellow followed him about just like a puppy. Why, he used to come right in here to see me, and I wish you could have seen the expression on his antelope face when he first walked across the slick linoleum. He looked so comical, just as though he'd like to say, 'My, my, what queer-feeling dirt you have in here! I can barely stand up!'

"And that ends the true story of Fluffy, an American pronghorn antelope who lived right here in the Hibbard yard," smiled George.

"Oh, I just loved that story," sighed Margaret Ann. "I wish you'd tell us another one. Won't you, please?"

"Yes, that surely was interesting, Mr. Hibbard," agreed Harold. "Now I've learned something else which I can pass along to my nature class at school. Thanks very much."

"You're both welcome," said George pleasantly. "But I think I'll have to beg off for today. A friend is coming by to take me for a ride, and I must get ready. But if you will come over again soon I'll be glad to visit with you."

"Good-by, and thank you again," Margaret Ann and Harold said as they went out the door. Harold called back, "And I'll be waiting to hear about the nest of gold."

With Another Ear-splitting Shriek the Great Engine Rushed Into
Sight and Started Toward the Trestle

CHAPTER 10

Terror on the Trestle

I'M SICK and tired of carrying all these clanking pots and pans around all over the country. Why can't Willie help out a little! Every morning after we have breakfast and put out our campfire, he finds some excuse for going on ahead." Harry glowered down at the rough seaside trail and wished for the hundredth time that he were an older brother who could do as he pleased.

"I'm tired too," moaned Ralph, shifting the big bedding roll over to the middle of his bicycle rack. "Just look at all the things my brother makes me carry. Why in the world did we buy all this food, anyway! We'll never be able to eat so much. Well, just you wait—some of these days I'll be as big as Willie, and then I'll let him carry his own things. Just see if I don't." He looked toward the third member of the group in time to see him nod in decided agreement.

Sunk in their gloomy self-pity, the three young boys, Jesse, Ralph, and Harry plodded sullenly along the future

Coastal Highway roadbed, blind to the breathtaking beauty of the rolling Pacific Ocean spread far out below them.

It had been about a week since the group had left their homes in Eugene and had started on the long-anticipated trip to the coast. There they planned to meet their friend Roy, whose father was owner of a large construction camp. Willie and Roy, who were older, had planned the excursion, and they had received many instructions from the fathers of the younger boys. For the first two or three days all had gone well, until the newness of their unaccustomed freedom had worn off. Then Willie had begun to travel with less and less equipment, and the three younger boys, much to their surprise, with more and more.

"We surely ought to reach that construction camp tonight," Jesse broke in. "Won't I be glad to get there and eat some of the cook's meals for a change! After a few breakfasts of Willie's pancakes I could eat shoe leather and call it good. Whoever told him that he could cook?"

Harry and Ralph grinned, in spite of their depression, and pushed their dusty bicycles forward a little faster.

"We're going to have to hurry if we catch up with him," puffed Ralph, as they guided their wheels up and down hill. "I want to get to camp as soon as he does, and then we'll have a chance to pick out our own bunks and not take what Willie and Roy think we should have. For once I'd like to get something besides the leftovers."

An hour or two went by, but still there was no sight of the older boy.

"Whew!" gasped Ralph, as they reached the summit

of a steep hill. "I'm going to have to sit down here awhile and rest. I'm all tired out."

"Oh, come on," urged Jesse, his dark hair ruffling in the stiff ocean breeze. "It can't be far now. Why, look down there! See? There's the railroad trestle that's being built. It's surely a long one. We'll have to cross it to get to the other side. The construction camp isn't very far away from there, I'm sure."

"Cross that?" asked Harry in amazement. "How are we going to wheel these loaded bikes across those bumpy ties? There's nothing else there except the steel rails and those little water barrel platforms sticking out along the side every few yards. Excuse me, but I'll get there some other way."

"How?" inquired practical Jesse. "There isn't any other way. That's the only road so far, so we'll either have to cross it, or go back home, and I for one am not going back home now." He stood up and lifted his bicycle with its load of clattering kettles. "Are you coming with me?"

"Pretty soon," groaned Ralph, rubbing his aching legs and tightening the buckles of his knee pants. "Harry and I will come along in a little while. I've got to rest first, though." He turned to his doubting friend, "We can make it all right, Harry. No trains'll be running yet over this new road. If we take our time, we'll get across safe and sound. Go ahead, Jesse. We'll catch up with you."

Slowly but surely Jesse inched his way across the huge, open railroad trestle, wheeling his bike carefully beside the shining steel rails. It made him dizzy to look down through the four-inch spaces between the ties and see the lapping waves far, far below. He was glad to rest at frequent intervals beside the tiny platforms that jutted out from the side of the rails. There was barely room for him to stand next to the water barrel and hold on to its edge to steady himself, but he was glad for even this chance of grasping a solid support.

At last he stepped off the narrow trestle. He heaved a deep sigh of relief as he turned and looked back over the quarter-mile crossing.

"Say, but I'm glad that's over," he muttered to himself. "I'd hate to go through that experience again. I'm still dizzy from walking between those rails."

He took out a crumpled red bandanna handkerchief and mopped his flushed face. As he restored it to his pocket he saw the faraway figures of Ralph and Harry just stepping out on the beginning of their perilous journey.

"Oh, oh," he thought sympathetically, "here they come. Look at Harry wobble along. He'd better be careful, or he'll fall off. What a splash *that* would make." He shivered as he eyed the great distance from the narrow trestle to the ocean inlet below. "Maybe I'd better leave my things here and go back to help him. Ralph'll make it—he's used to climbing tall trees, and he doesn't get dizzy—but Harry's scared. I can tell that!"

Jesse leaned his wheel against a tall clump of golden Scotchbroom and started back toward his friends. He had walked about a block when he first heard the faraway sound.

"Ooooooo-ooo. Oooooooooo-oooo," it echoed mournfully.

Again the startled boy heard the mournful wail.

"Oooooo-ooo. Ooooooooo-oooo!"

"Get off the track!" it seemed to shriek. "Get off the track. I'm c-o-o-o-o-o-ming! I'm c-o-o-o-o-o-ming!"

"The train!" Jesse yelled to Ralph and Harry, who were now exactly halfway across the bridge. "The train's coming. Drop your bikes. Run for your lives."

Then he turned and ran back to his bicycle beside the Scotchbroom. As he hurled himself off the trestle he heard the clattering of the train wheels around the bend.

"They'll never make it," Jesse gasped. He cupped his hands around his mouth and yelled with all his strength.

"Drop your bikes over the edge. Drop them, I say. And run. Run!"

Louder and louder roared the onrushing train. With another earsplitting shriek the great engine rushed into sight and started toward the trestle. Bells clanged as the engineer waved wildly at the boys to save themselves.

Jesse could not turn his horrified look from Ralph and Harry. He could not speak. He could not call out. All he could do was to stand, terrified, to watch his best friends fall beneath the grinding wheels of the monster. And then his heart gave a leap as his eyes fell upon the small water barrel platforms that had afforded welcome resting places during his crossing. It was a chance in a million, but it might work.

"Get on the platform!" he screamed, jumping up and down and pointing toward the nearest one. "Get on the platform!" His words were drowned in the great rush of the approaching gravel train, but his gestures could be seen and understood. And Ralph, stumbling desperately ahead of Harry, understood Jesse's frantic motions.

Jesse's frightened eyes saw Ralph lurch forward in one great jump. He saw him grasp the water barrel with one hand while he clutched his bicycle with the other, pulling and tugging until it hung over the edge beside him. There it swayed back and forth, high above the rolling tide far below. And just at that instant the train thundered by, sparks flying from beneath the wheels, smoke belching from the smokestack. On, on, the iron wheels hurtled, flashing past Ralph and toward Harry.

But just then Jesse saw that Harry, too, now clung to the safety of another water barrel and that his bicycle also dangled far out over the platform's edge.

Weak with relief, Jesse watched the shaking, trembling boys inch their way across the intervening space. As soon as they reached the road they fell flat upon the ground, and there they lay for some time.

"Was that a narrow escape!" Jesse blurted, when he had regained his breath. "I was never so scared as when I heard that train whistle."

"Scared!" exclaimed Ralph. "My knees were nothing but jelly. I don't know how in the world I ever got out onto that platform."

"Me, either," wheezed Harry. "All I can remember is seeing that train bearing down on me. Then somehow I saw you waving, Jesse, and all at once I was out on a platform, just like Ralph. Oh, but I was frightened!"

It was some time before the three youthful adventurers felt strong enough to continue the short remaining distance to the camp. But at length they arrived there, to be greeted by Roy, his father, and the camp cook—who listened with interest to their exciting adventure.

In the following hours, as they became the center of attention for the returning work crews, they quite forgot their early morning grievance toward Willie and Roy. In fact, they almost felt sorry for the two older boys, who were completely unnoticed and in the background during the entire evening while the men complimented the boys on their quick thinking.

"Maybe it's a good thing to be a younger brother sometimes," grinned Jesse early that night, as he and Ralph and Harry curled up in the best bunks in the bunkhouse. "At least this is one time when being left behind with all the pots and pans and bedding proved to be exciting."

"That may be," agreed Harry, "but as far as I'm concerned you can have all the railroad trestles you want. I wouldn't go through that experience again for a million dollars. I'll gladly leave my share of all those supplies right here for the camp rather than carry them back across that trestle. I told you we'd never be able to use all that food we brought along. We certainly don't need it here, where all our meals are furnished."

"Well, cheer up," grinned Ralph. "We can take our supplies back with us and use them when we go camping up the McKenzie River. Our good friend the cook said that he could arrange for us to ride back to Eugene in the gravel train. That'll be a lot easier than bicycling 125 miles. Won't it be fun to load everything into the caboose and then just sit back and rest?"

"Three cheers!" shouted Jesse. "Three cheers for the cook and the gravel train."

CHAPTER 11

Fire in the Night

"DARLENE, will you please answer the telephone for me? I'm busy right now," called mother from the kitchen. "See who it is, and tell them I'll be right there."

Darlene put down the handful of silverware with which she was setting the table and hurriedly picked up the receiver.

"Hello. Oh, yes, Mrs. Thompson. Why, I think I could, but I'll have to ask mother first. May I call you in a few minutes, or do you want to wait while I find out? All right, I'll let you know right away."

Darlene hung up the receiver and rushed into the kitchen, her eyes shining with delight. "Mother, guess what Mrs. Thompson wants! Just guess! No, let me tell you instead. She wants me—ME—to come over this evening and stay with the children while she and Mr. Thompson go out. She said that Evelyn had a cold and couldn't be there, and so she thought she'd call me. Now I'll get to help put the baby to bed and tell Judy a good-night story. Please let me go, Mother. We've been over there visiting so many times that I'm sure I'll know just what to do."

She watched breathlessly until mother spoke; then her face clouded with disappointment at the answer.

"I'm sorry, dear, but I'd rather not let you go. It's a school night, and you need your ten hours' sleep. The Thompsons don't have a free evening very often, and I imagine that they'll stay out rather late. This would mean that you would have to stay awake, for you sleep so soundly that you'd never hear the children if you went to bed. You're only eleven; when you are older, there'll be plenty of time for baby sitting. But it was nice of Mrs. Thompson to telephone. It shows that she has confidence in you and believes you to be trustworthy."

"But, Mother," wailed Darlene, "you just don't understand. They aren't going out for pleasure. Mr. Thompson's sister is quite sick and they have to go 'way over on the other side of town to see her and take some medicine and things that she needs. Mrs. Thompson said she wouldn't have asked me otherwise, because she knew I went to bed early."

"Well, that does put a different face on the matter," mother briskly replied. "I'll call Mrs. Thompson myself. If it's an emergency, we should do what we can to help."

At seven-thirty Darlene settled herself comfortably in a large rocker in the Thompson home and opened her new Junior Reading Course book. Two-year-old Judy and four-month-old Tony had been lovingly tucked in their cribs, and their parents had just left, promising to be back as soon as possible.

"I'm sure that you'll be warm, dear," Mrs. Thompson had said. "Dan stoked the new furnace about an hour ago, so you won't need to do a thing with the heating plant. The children sleep soundly; just look in their room a time or two to see that they are well covered. Other than that there is nothing for you to do but just be here. We'll leave Cookie; she's a good little watchdog and will keep you company until we return."

Although this was Darlene's first experience as nursemaid in sole charge, she found it a pleasant one. For an hour she read without interruption, and then stopped only because her eyes began to feel heavy.

"Eight-thirty!" she exclaimed to the red cocker spaniel, who for the past few minutes had been padding restlessly toward the door and back again. "It's eight-thirty already, and half-an-hour past my usual bedtime. No wonder I'm getting sleepy."

She rubbed her eyes with the back of one hand as she listened to the little click-click of Cookie's toenails on the hardwood floor.

"Oh, lie down, Cookie. What's wrong with you! You make me nervous when you prowl around that way. Lie down over here by me like a good dog. Come on."

But, coax as she would, Cookie would not lie down. Back and forth she walked, first toward one door and then toward another.

"I do believe you want me to go in and look at the children. Is that it?" Darlene spoke aloud, smiling down at the nervous little pet. "Come along with me, then. We'll see if Judy and Tony are covered up."

Together they quietly entered the bedroom to find

that all was well; the little tots were sound asleep and well covered. Darlene was amused at the way the cocker spaniel carefully sniffed at the bed covers and poked her black nose into each corner of the room.

Again Darlene settled herself in the big chair, but this time it was much harder to keep awake. In fact, several times she dozed and then sat up with a jerk that hurt her neck. At last she felt as though she couldn't stay awake another second. "I'll just close my eyes for one minute," she afterward recalled thinking. "It'll rest them after so much reading." And that was the last she knew until she heard Cookie's frantic bark and felt the dog's cold nose repeatedly nudging her hand.

"Bow-wow," barked Cookie. "Bow-wow-wow!" Over and over she signaled, dog fashion, running back and forth between Darlene and the closed door. The cocker's eyes were wide with excitement; she seemed to be doing her best to tell Darlene something of great importance.

Darlene's sleepy eyes just barely opened as she staggered drowsily to her feet. "What in the world is wrong with you, Cookie?" she asked almost crossly. "The children are all right. It hasn't been very long since we were in there to look at them."

As she spoke she looked at the clock. Instantly she was jolted wide awake. Eleven o'clock! Surely something must have happened to delay the Thompsons. Why, even on Saturday night she was seldom allowed to stay up until eleven o'clock, and on a school night it was an unheard-of event. What would mother say! Well, she knew that it meant that never again could she stay at the Thompsons as a baby sitter, although she could often

She Had No More Than Flung Open the Living Room Door
Than She Knew the Answer to Cookie's Restlessness,
for Suddenly She Smelled Smoke

come with mother to pay a friendly call and play with the babies. They were such darlings. How she loved to play with Judy and wheel little Tony out in the yard.

"Bow-wow-wow," again barked Cookie, looking desperately toward the door.

"All right, all right," Darlene said. "Come on. We'll go across the hall together."

She had no more than flung open the living room door than she knew the answer to Cookie's restlessness. For suddenly she smelled smoke. She could not tell from what direction it came, but it was unmistakably smoke.

"It must be from the new furnace that Mr. Thompson just put in," she thought, hurrying toward the nursery. "After I look at Judy and Tony I suppose I should go down to the furnace, but I wouldn't know what to do if anything was wrong. Oh, dear. I wish the folks would come home."

As her hand reached for the doorknob Cookie's barking rose to a loud crescendo. Instantly Darlene gasped and jerked away her fingers. A chill ran down her back as she stared at the door. She listened intently. What was that? Again she listened carefully. Then she heard it very distinctly—a tiny crackling noise that whitened her cheeks and started her knees trembling.

Without an instant's hesitation she grasped the knob and flung open the door. A burst of flame and smoke shot out into the hall. Darlene shrank back in horror. Cookie stood stanchly by her side, hair bristling, white teeth showing as she snarled.

"Oh, oh, the whole room's on fire," sobbed Darlene, wringing her hands. "What shall I do! The babies are in

8

there. They'll be burned to death. And the fire's spread-
ing—it'll burn the whole house down. Oh, what can I
do!"

She started toward the doorway, only to be met with
another burst of smoke and flame. She heard Tony's
cough and Judy's answering cry. She must get them. She
must! But how?

As she looked down at the frantic little dog she
noticed for the first time the heavy handmade wool rug
upon which she stood. "I wonder——" she thought. "If
I put this over my head, could I get into the room? I
mustn't breathe the smoke, or I'll die. But I must go in
there and get them out now, or it'll be too late."

Instantly Darlene stooped and jerked up the new hall
rug of which Mrs. Thompson was so proud. Quickly she
threw it over her head and shoulders. She looked in the
direction of the two little beds, side by side. And then,
taking a deep breath, she plunged desperately into the
terrific heat. Cookie ran by her side, barking loudly. At
once Darlene smelled the singeing hair upon the little pet
as Cookie brushed against a smoldering baseboard. Stoop-
ing, so as not to dislodge her covering, she grabbed Judy,
who clung desperately around her neck. Then she
snatched up limp little Tony and, guided by Cookie's
barking, groped her way into the hall, which was even
then beginning to blaze.

On and on the two little figures struggled through
the fire and smoke. On and on, until at last they staggered
across the porch and out onto the lawn, where Darlene
fell in a heap, releasing her precious burden. As she
flung off the charring rug and stamped on it, she heard

the loud crash of the bedroom wall as it fell in upon the very spot where such a short time before two little babies had been sound asleep.

"I'm sorry I burned up your nice new rug," Darlene said soberly to Mrs. Thompson the next day, as she lay, bandaged like a mummy, in her bed at home.

"Oh, my dear child," cried Mrs. Thompson, tears in her pretty eyes. "What is a rug or a house or anything in the world compared to our loved ones? You'll never know what a dreadful shock it was when we returned home to find firemen and neighbors gathered about the part of our house left standing, but no sign of any children at all.

"Until you are grown, with a family of your own, you will never realize how grateful we are to you. If Evelyn had come, she and our children would surely have died in the fire, for she has always fallen asleep early in the evening, and has not awakened until our return. It was only because you awoke from your doze and heard Cookie's warning that your lives were spared. Faithful little dog, she's going to be all right, too, as soon as her paws are healed. And don't forget that both of you will have a suitable reward for your bravery.

"But we mustn't talk any more now. No one knows how the fire started, but our house was well insured and we can rebuild. The most important thing, however, is that everyone was saved and that you are going to be all right." She smiled tearfully up at mother.

"Yes, the doctor says that the burns, while painful, will heal over smoothly," mother answered. "I, too, am devoutly thankful that the lives of our dear ones were spared. And I am also very proud that my daughter remembered her responsibility toward those in her care. That is something that is to me the best reward of all!"

Darlene tried to smile, although the effort was a painful one. But smile she did as she said, "Well, all I can say is this: I don't think that any other baby sitter I ever heard about had as much excitement as I did on my very first night. I hope that my next baby-sitting job is a little more quiet and peaceful!"

"I Don't Think Any Other Baby Sitter I Ever Heard About Had as Much Excitement as I Did on My Very First Night"

CHAPTER 12

Roundup
From the Sky

I'D CERTAINLY like to see a real cowboy while I'm visiting over here at Grandma Grace's," said Marilyn. She stretched out on the green lawn and began to look for four-leaf clovers.

"So would I! And maybe I could ride on his horse. Wouldn't that be fun?" added seven-year-old Stephen Joel. His brown eyes sparkled at the thought of riding a prancing pony down the main street of Burns.

"What does a cowboy look like, anyway?" he questioned his sister.

"Oh, he's a man who wears a silk shirt with a bright bandanna neckerchief and big woolly chaps and a big hat and—oh, yes—high-heeled cowboy boots with pointed toes and silver spurs that jangle when he walks."

"Ho!" sneered Cedric. "Isn't that just like a girl! What a foolish idea! A cowboy doesn't look like that at all."

"He does too," stoutly maintained Marilyn. "I know

he does, because I've seen magazine pictures of cowboys, and they were dressed exactly that way."

"Maybe you've seen such photographs, Miss Smarty, but those weren't real buckaroos. Those were just dude ranch folks all dressed up to impress their city guests. Real cowboys out here on the range ride hard and work long hours. And they wear plain shirts, with tight-fitting, belted overalls, and old weatherbeaten hats. They *do* wear high-heeled boots, but only because that kind fit best into the stirrups—not for looks."

Marilyn and Stephen looked so crestfallen that Grandpa Jim got up out of his porch rocker and joined the quarreling children.

"Here, here," he smiled. "Let's settle the argument in a friendly way. Cedric's right about the buckaroo and his horse, youngsters, but even at that he hasn't described the very latest style in cowboy travel. Your grandmother and I are going out on the Bend Highway on an errand. Do you want to go with us and meet a modern cowboy?"

Grandpa and Grandma Lampshire laughed heartily at the speed with which their grandchildren clambered into the back of the Chevrolet pick-up truck.

"Hold on tight!" Grandpa called, "and don't lean out over the sides. Here we go."

A few blocks beyond the outskirts of the town he turned the truck off the highway and toward a small, tree-shaded house that sat companionably near a large building.

"I wonder why we're stopping here?" Marilyn asked the boys. "I don't see any horses out in the fields near by."

Cedric shrugged his shoulders, and Stephen's happy face clouded over with disappointment.

"Where's that cowboy we're going to see, Grandpa Jim? And where's his horse?" he asked, as his grandfather opened the cab door.

"Jump out, all of you," smiled Grandpa Jim. "Come along with us and you'll soon find out."

As they followed the Lampshires up the path, Stephen whispered to Marilyn.

"Maybe he keeps all his horses shut up in that big shed right over there. I imagine that's where all of them are. Don't you think so?"

But just then a sweet-faced young woman greeted them at the door, and in the midst of all the introductions Marilyn's answer was lost.

"So these are your young visitors for the summer," Mrs. Roe Davis said, as she smiled at the children. "Come right in. My daughters, Lola and Mildred, will be especially glad to meet you, for some years ago they studied piano from your mother, when she taught school over here.

"You arrived at the right time, for they and their father have just come in from a morning ride down to the White Horse Ranch. Roe had to go there to locate a band of horses, and urged all of us to ride with him. However, I couldn't spare the time from needed household tasks. Yesterday we rode down to Cottage Grove, and tomorrow we're going to Boise, Idaho."

White Horse Ranch—Cottage Grove, Oregon—Boise, Idaho—Cedric's head began to spin as he mentally calculated the distance of each trip. That historic old stage-coach stop, the White Horse Ranch in the south end of Harney County, was many hours' journey by car from Burns, as were the two cities.

"Then you'll have ridden hundreds of miles in less than three days!" he puzzled. "I don't see how you could do it and still be back here this early, even with a new car."

"New car!" interrupted Marilyn. "Why, he doesn't even use a car. Does he, Mrs. Davis? He must be the cowboy that Grandpa Jim told us we were coming to see, and so I'm sure he'd ride horseback. But I—well, I don't understand how any horses could go that far in two or three days."

"Well, well, so you're wondering about my horses," laughed Mr. Davis good-naturedly. He shook hands with everyone and then sat down with Stephen on his knee. "Would you like to see what carries me so swiftly over the country?"

Stephen nodded his head and smiled shyly up at the friendly speaker.

"Is he white? I guess he must be, if you got him at the White Horse Ranch when you went down to look at those horses. Could I see him now, please?"

"Of course you may. Come along, all of you."

Stephen and Marilyn clasped hands tightly as they skipped along to the large building.

"Just think! Now we're really going to see what they look like," whispered the little boy to his sister. "And I'm going to ask if I can ride on that white pony. Maybe he'll let me. He seems awfully nice."

But the children's wide eyes saw no horses of any

kind in that large building. For when Mr. Davis opened the doors, they saw, instead of horses, several shiny airplanes.

"Oh, oh!" exclaimed Cedric, grinning sheepishly. "I understand now. I should have known what you meant when you talked about traveling so far in such a short time. But Grandpa Jim kept talking about a modern cowboy, you see, and naturally I didn't even think about airplanes."

"But—but I want to see a horse," burst forth Stephen, his mouth drooping. "I've seen lots of airplanes."

"Well, perhaps you've seen many planes, but you've never seen anyone use a plane as Roe Davis does," said Grandma Grace. "Perhaps he'll tell you about his work while I talk to Mrs. Davis for a few minutes."

"Oh, please do tell us," begged Marilyn, as they returned to the house and sat down. "I'd certainly like to know how you can be called a cowboy when you don't even ride horseback."

"Well, it's quite a long story," smiled Mr. Davis, "but I'll try to give you the main facts, partly as outlined in *Newsweek* magazine and partly as I can recall other experiences of interest to you.

"Some writers have called me a 'modern cowhand,' a sort of flying handyman who helps the many ranchers in the high desert country of southeastern Oregon. I've done several things, from sowing seed for the farmers and hunting coyotes with plane and shotgun, to rounding up herds of wild horses.

"About three years ago my partner, Bill Stevens, and I began hunting coyotes in my Piper Cub. We first began

We Fly About 150 Feet Above the Ground to Locate the Coyote.
When We See Him We Come Down to Only About 20 Feet

working for some sheepmen, who hired us by the hour. Later on, the price of coyote pelts rose to fifteen dollars apiece, and in 1943 we bagged more than four hundred pelts. By the time prices had dropped we still had employment of the same type, for the Oregon Game Commission hired three teams of pilots and gunners to destroy these prairie wolves which prey upon cattle and game. In February, which is the mating season, Bill and I bagged 137 coyotes in fifty-seven hours.

"I was the pilot, and Bill was the gunner, using a shotgun loaded with BB shot. We found that coyote hunting by air was the most successful over the sagebrush range at a height of about five hundred feet. At that height the tracks of rabbits, deer, and coyotes can best be seen in the snow."

"Can you really see the coyote plainly, Mr. Davis?" breathlessly asked Marilyn.

"Indeed we can," nodded the cowboy-pilot. "Coyotes run about twenty-five miles an hour and usually travel in pairs or families. They run in packs from the last of December to the first part of February, which, as I have already told you, is the coyote mating season.

"Sometimes we have seen as many as eleven coyotes in a pack. We watch, and try to locate them at their dens in the sagebrush up the little ravines. They often choose a shallow badger hole from three to six feet back in the top of a little hill, because they don't care much about digging out the dens themselves.

"We fly about 150 feet above the ground to locate the coyote. When we see him we come down to a distance of only twenty feet above the ground, as when pelt hunting we hunt mostly in open country where we can land for a pickup, and take off again."

"You mean you save the animal's fur?" cried Stephen. "How can you stop to pick up the coyote?"

"Indeed we save the pelt," smiled the pilot. "If we're on wheels, we land about a quarter of a mile away, or, if the landing place is not suitable, we just let the prairie wolf run until we can shoot and then land. But when the snow is good, we fly on skis. Here is a picture showing the plane on skis and three of the coyotes killed at that time."

"Does your gunner always kill the animals? Or do any of the wounded ones try to attack you?" breathlessly questioned Cedric.

"Bill's a mighty good shot, missing only about one in every five shots," answered Mr. Davis. "He has to shoot from the left side of the plane, too, with time for only one shot. If this misses, the plane has to take a long sweep and come back for a second run. Whenever he sees a pair he tries to kill the male first, for the female will stay beside the body of her mate. But if the female is killed first, the male tries to run away.

"And, by the way, I heard an interesting fact as to how the male coyote cares for the young ones if the female is killed. I can't verify this statement but I was told that the male will go out to hunt, will eat the food, and will then from his stomach return this predigested food for the pups. At the age of seven weeks the pups are able to eat solid food.

"But to get back to your question, Cedric," he continued, "I can say that I've had a few exciting experiences in which a wounded animal tried to attack me. One old fellow became pretty wise after escaping two plane runs. We had quite a time when he began dodging us instead of running straight ahead. But at last Bill shot him, wounding him. After we had landed on skis, I began to follow the trail, and came suddenly upon the animal. Instead of being afraid, he started savagely toward me, and I had to shoot him with my pistol. At another time we saw an enraged coyote actually turn at bay and try to attack the airplane as we passed over him. Lola, will you please hand us that picture taken by Mr. Meyers? It's really a very unusual photograph." The children, their heads together, gazed at the picture.

"Ugh!" cried Marilyn. "It seems cruel to kill the poor things. I should think you'd hate to."

"No, you wouldn't, Marilyn, if you could see how savage these creatures become," Mr. Davis continued soberly. "They show no pity for harmless animals, and will kill young deer and antelope, as well as calves and lambs.

"At one time I watched two coyotes stalking two deer: a doe and her tiny fawn. One wily old coyote kept the brave mother deer busy by repeatedly rushing at her from the front while the second coyote sneaked in behind to try to kill the helpless little fawn. Both of the beasts were big fellows, and even in ten inches of snow they could have kept up these tactics until the mother deer was completely exhausted. Then they planned to rush in and hamstring the deer—cut the muscles in her hind legs so that her legs would give way. After that she would be unable to defend herself or her fawn. We didn't wait for this to happen. We shot those two coyotes right then and there.

"I've seen them try the same tactics in spring lambing time, stalking an old ewe with her lamb snuggled right up against her. Coyotes are more destructive at this time of year than at any other, because the lambs and calves are small then and unable to defend themselves.

"These prairie wolves also rob the nests of ducks and geese, and eat the young ones. After the lake freezes over, they will paw open muskrat houses that stick up out of the ice. In fact, a woman at one of the bird refuge headquarters called me one day to come by plane and shoot a sly old coyote who sneaked into her barnyard every morning and carried away a fat chicken for his breakfast."

"I still can't see how you can bring home all those coyotes in that little plane," interrupted Marilyn, with a puzzled frown. "I wouldn't think you'd have room for all of them."

"That's a good question, Dad," laughed Lola. "You forgot to tell the children how you do that."

"In the wintertime we can land on skis and skin a coyote in four or five minutes," replied Mr. Davis. "To do this, we cut down the hind legs, skin the hind legs and tail, and then pull off his hide. Thus at night we would come in with from eight to eighteen or nineteen hides. The biggest catch we had was twenty-two coyotes in one day.

"The next procedure is to stretch the hides on boards —just as fox pelts are treated—one night turning the pelts with the fur in, and the next night turning the pelts with the fur out. Sometimes it is necessary to do some scraping for fat, but not often. Then the pelts dry for a week."

"I'm sorry to interrupt this conversation," said Grandpa Jim, "but it's time that we were on our way, for I have an appointment within half an hour. Yes, I know that you hate to leave, but perhaps Mr. Davis will tell you more about his hunting some other time."

"Oh, will you, please?" chorused the three interested listeners as they reluctantly rose to go.

"Of course, I'll be glad to," nodded Mr. Davis. "In fact, I was just getting nicely started. I hadn't even gotten as far as the large antelope herds we see, or the wild horses that we round up by plane, driving them up the hills into a little draw, where they are run down a chute into trucks. That also is an interesting story."

"Dad," broke in Mildred, "perhaps the youngsters would like several of these pictures to take along with them. Here's one that shows you in front of your airplane with 158 coyote hides—part of your winter's catch."

"We'd surely like to have them," replied Cedric. "And thank you so much for the story. I'd surely like to have a chance to see some of those wild horses you mentioned."

"Well, Cedric, I'll be busy for the next week or so, but perhaps sometime after that you can ride with me when I go down toward Catlow Valley. You'll see really wild horses down there, all right, and I'll show you how we round them up by plane.

"Wait a minute before you go," he added. "I have a present for each of you. I'll be right back."

"What do you suppose it can be?" Stephen whispered curiously to Marilyn.

"I can't imagine," she replied softly, shaking her head. "I expect it's another picture, though."

But Mr. Davis did not return with another picture. The youngsters gasped with delight when they saw the present that he handed to them, and each one said, "Oh, thank you, Mr. Davis," with heartfelt sincerity.

"I thought you'd like these soft coyote furs," he stated. "They make fine rugs for bedside use, and they'll last a long time. Now you'll remember my story each morning when you jump out of bed, for you'll step out on one of the coyotes that was rounded up by plane."

"Wasn't that fun, Stephen?" questioned Marilyn, as they drove away from the Davis home.

"It certainly was," agreed Stephen, clinging to the car with one hand and his precious coyote skin with the other. "We didn't see any horses, but this was even better, because I couldn't keep a horse in my bedroom, but I can keep a coyote rug by my bed."

"And am I lucky!" bragged Cedric. "Just think. Maybe I'm going to get to go with Mr. Davis in his Piper Cub. Won't Edwin wish he'd come over with us on our trip? Just wait till I go back and tell my big brother that I met a modern cowhand and rode with him over the eastern Oregon range on his roundup from the sky!"

We'd love to have you download our catalog of titles we publish at:

www.TEACHServices.com

or write or email us your thoughts, reactions, or criticism about this or any other book we publish at:

TEACH Services, Inc.
254 Donovan Road
Brushton, NY 12916

info@TEACHServices.com

or you may call us at:

518/358-3494

Produced in partnership with
LNFBooks.com